I0546102

BLOOD

BRIDE

Belle Blukat

WolfSinger Publications ⸾ Security, Colorado

Copyright © 2022 by Dana Bell
Published by WolfSinger Publications

Cover Art copyright 2022 © Lee Ann Barlow

ISBN 978-1-944637-13-2

Printed and bound in the United States of America

Acknowledgements

I have a few people to thank for this book and for their contributions to the story.

Carol Hightshoe and Julie Campbell for helping pick names for the cats.

Sarah Levesque for beta reading the novel, making suggestions, and asking questions that helped make this book a much better one.

Kessie Carroll for her suggestion about the role the hunters should play, which provided an unusual twist to their relationship with the vampires.

Dedication

This book is dedicated to God
who inspired this story and helped me write it in two months.

To Adara, who passed away in April of 2021, and to Taj,
both of whom inspired the cat characters

TABLE OF CONTENTS

Chapter 1
The Con Friday

"Hey, Cira!"

Great. I stopped and turned my attention toward the main registration table littered with programs, various items for sale and a stack of lanyards, the faint smell of chlorine reaching my nose from the inside pool. One of the volunteers waved me over wearing the normal bright green 'Staff' T-shirt.

"Could you do us a favor and take our Science Guest of Honor here," she nodded at the tall, and, I have to admit, good-looking middle-aged man, standing there with a lost expression on his red bearded face. "Up to where participants and guests check in?" Her round face gave me a hopeful look.

"Sure. I'm headed up there myself." In fact, I was running a bit late, or felt like I was. It had been one of those days. I hoped I would make my first panel on time. Needed to check in first to make certain I knew which room it was being held in.

"Thanks!" She turned her attention to the next person in the already long line filled with folks wearing everything from jeans and T-shirts of their favorite shows or movies or fandom to those in beautifully handmade costumes.

"Dr. Bertram Hoel," my charge introduced himself stepping away. He looked like the typical college professor wearing a brown tweed jacket and dress pants. The Scientist extended his hand.

"Cira Landon. I'm one of the local writers." I took his hand, noting the odd chill.

"Pleasure to meet you." He lifted my hand and lightly kissed it.

Okay, that's great in romance in novels, but who in real life kisses a woman's hand outside of actors at the Ren Faire? Secretly, I loved it and felt a bit of thrill at the touch of his lips.

"You as well," I managed after staring into those amazing golden-brown eyes. Shaking my head, I reclaimed my hand and motioned. "This way."

We walked across the hotel lobby. I've been here many times through the years. Granted, there had been changes. Today the white tile gleamed and the hotel employees in their smart blue uniforms and gold name badges smiled, checking in guests, despite the oddly dressed fans wandering about.

"I hear this is your first Science Fiction Convention." Or so rumor said. I hoped what I'd heard proved correct and I hadn't just made a fool of myself.

"I've had many invitations. This is the first I've accepted." He had an odd accent. Not quite British, but close.

"Why is that?" I had to gather up my long blue skirt as we started up the dark brown marbled stairs to reach the second floor.

"I'm usually traveling. This is not my first visit to the Mile High City, although I will admit it has changed."

Right. World renowned scientist in astronomy, biology and other fields according to his bio in the con program. He'd consulted with NASA and was friends with well-known international leaders in more countries than I would get the chance to visit in my lifetime. "You enjoy traveling?" I asked looking for a way to talk to Dr. Hoel.

"I did when I was younger." Briefly he looked very tired. I noticed a few wrinkles around his eyes and streaks of gray scattered in his light reddish-brown hair. "I'm starting to enjoy the comforts of being home more."

"I miss traveling." Hadn't been able to do much since my ex-husband Paul walked out on me a few years back. Thinking of him made me cringe. He'd be at the convention during the weekend and I had been trying to figure out how to avoid him. The man suffered from the delusion we were still friends. Personally, I wanted nothing to do with him. Not after the way he'd treated me while we were married.

"Why are you sad?"

"What?" I glanced at the scientist.

We'd reached the second floor. My fingers smoothed the satin fabric. I'd spent many hours working on my Victorian costume and wanted it to look good.

"You seemed sad." His eyes searched my face. "I wondered why."

"Nothing important." There are times I hate being an empath. I could tell he felt concerned, yet underneath it I could sense he was a man used to holding and wielding power. And below that, an almost predatory nature that I found unnerving. "The line is here." I pointed at the straggling group waiting to check in. I recognized my fellow authors, several local artists and the normal con folks who helped run panels or other events.

"Thank you." He gave me a slight bow and waved his hand. "After you."

I nodded graciously and took my place, checking my phone for the time, glad to see I shouldn't have a problem making my panel before it started.

Dr. Hoel turned to visit with one of my long-time friends Dan Palma, an astronomer at a well-known observatory in Arizona as well as an up-and-coming Science Fiction writer. I had a panel with him on Saturday.

"Parties can start now, I have arrived!" echoed from across the cathedral ceiling.

Inwardly I groaned yet managed to offer the man who'd just arrived a smile and greeted him with a hug. "I heard you were coming Tom. Do you really have to make an entrance?" I teased him.

"Of course!" He grinned impishly at me. One of the most brilliant men I knew, and he rarely dressed up for anything. Today proved no exception. Ripped jeans and a T-shirt proclaiming his loyalty to a show we all loved, which had been cancelled by short sighted network executives. I'd bet they were still scratching their heads over why the program had a huge cult following.

I decided to make introductions. "Tom, meet Dr. Bertram Hoel. Dr. Hoel, Tom William Canyon. I believe you two are on some of the same panels." I'd checked the schedule online earlier and had noted who was on what.

The two men shook hands. "Nice to meet you, Dr. Hoel," Tom greeted, his quick friendly smile offered. Hard to believe he had gray at his temples making his short black curly hair stand out.

"Mr. Canyon."

"Mr. Canyon was my father. Just call me Tom."

"Tom," Dr. Hoel agreed.

They lapsed into a conversation filled with scientific jargon and I knew I could ignore them. Finally reaching the small registration desk, I got my badge, program book and made a hasty exit to go downstairs. I knew I'd bump into friends on my way to my panel room. We normally greeted each other with hugs and quick catch-up conversations. Some folks I maybe saw once or twice a year.

As I reached the stairs, I glanced back and noticed Dr. Hoel's eyes following me. A man hadn't looked at me with interest for several years. It both thrilled me and made me very nervous.

~ * ~

Normally Bertram ignored women after he'd met them. Many had taken an interest in him for his influential position and the perception he had money. Truthfully, he did, yet he refused to live any way other than modestly when traveling. His tactic discouraged the opposite sex from chasing after him and he preferred it that way.

Granted he would enjoy a lovely neck now and again, his mouth watering at the thought of tasting their hot sweet blood. He'd have to be careful to when or who he hunted. No need to start rumors among those who probably read or even wrote vampire novels. His kind safely lived on the written page or in films. He had no wish to shatter the illusion.

He gave the green shirted volunteer a smile as he clipped his badge on his jacket pocket. With a nod he parted from Tom and decided to check out the hotel layout so he could make his panels on time.

On the upper level he found the rooms for the art show, the dealer's room, main events space and a smattering of tables full of authors and artists selling their work. Several were setting up, smiling and chatting with each other.

The lower level contained more tables for groups, the panel rooms, and a couple where various movies, cartoons and TV shows would be shown during the weekend.

He wondered which room the lovely Cira Landon occupied. With a frown he chided himself on why it should possibly be important, yet their brief encounter had left an impression on him. Closing his eyes, he recalled her image. Tanned oval face with gray eyes touched with carefully concealed sadness. Long dark hair, whether brown or black he couldn't be certain. Part of it had been braided back and secured with a sparkling barrette. He'd guess she was maybe in her forties, perhaps a bit older. The blue dress she wore complimented her figure and with a smile he speculated what it would be like to put his arms around her.

Thoughts like that could be dangerous and he shook himself, trying to force his mind away from the attractive woman who had drawn his attention. The best way to protect his nature—do not become involved too closely with anyone. Yes, he had a few select friends in Boston, the city he called home. Some were like him, others hired for their special talents and paid well to keep their silence or a hunter who owed him a favor.

His eyes drifted watching the attendees, some in jeans and T-shirts, others in carefully made costumes. In the center sat a big blue box and as he remembered, it served as the spaceship for a British program. While he kept himself familiar with popular culture, for the most part he didn't indulge in the various fan driven activities.

His own interests lay in the arena of science itself and he'd spent his last two centuries attending various universities and collecting as many doctorates as possible. He'd lost count of how many he held and from where. Bertram loved learning and would continue pursuing it as if were a woman to be won.

When had been the last time he'd truly won a woman? He didn't mean the casual hookups for the purpose of securing their blood. Rather the art of winning a woman's heart for the purpose of romance and other pleasures. Pleasures he'd long denied himself. He could not recall the last time he'd bedded a woman.

Isaac, one of the few among their kind who had married and transformed his bride, being slightly older than Bertram, often told him not to ignore the desires he had. Not that he'd listened or even considered his maker's suggestion until now.

Maybe the fates had brought Cira into his path to tempt him away from his education mistress. He certainly found his thoughts traveling down paths he had long ignored. Yet a relationship with a human had often proven a treacherous trail and he'd seen many taken down by hunters, who used lovely women as bait. Part of why the Elders had made peace with them over a century ago.

Bertram couldn't afford to make the same mistake with Cira no matter how drawn to her he felt. Should Martelli, one with whom he'd once been friends before their falling out, discover he cared for a woman, her fate could be far worse.

~ * ~

Luckily, I managed to be on time for my panel. Taking my place at the end of the long table I pulled out my water bottle and stuffed furred friend. I took one with me to every con. This one I'd named Rowdy, the lovely, if somewhat ornery gray and white wolf. She wore a ruby collar and her brown eyes accused me of trying to make her into an ordinary dog. Not true of course.

"Hey, Cira," Lisa Jacobs greeted me, taking the chair next to mine, her long brown hair braided down her back, and her matching eyes twinkling. She wore a bright rainbow-colored outfit, complete with a horse mane and tail.

"How's your newest series doing?" I asked. She wrote amazing horse and dog books.

"Not bad," she answered, stacking a few copies of her titles in front of her.

"No dog today?" She usually brought one of her collies for one or all three days.

"Maybe tomorrow. Ran late at work and didn't have time to pick 'em up."

"I look forward to seeing them." One of the ways I got my dog fix. My cats wouldn't be happy since they think they own me. They'd consider it a betrayal.

"Make sure you come by my table. I have a few new titles out."

"I'll be by." I normally bought at least one or two of her newest releases.

The other two panelists came in. One was our Guest of Honor, Conner Douglas, who had written several best sellers about dragons. Looked the part too, complete with a gray cloak, a pointed wizard hat, and holding a wooden staff.

Last, but not least, another up and comer, Bruce Sheridan. His specialty—vampire novels. Self-published, a great salesman and dressed all in black leather with silver chains hanging around his neck, one of which of course, was a cross.

I chuckled. Vampires were supposed to be afraid of crosses, although an argument could be made for fearing whatever their holy sign was, depending on where they lived and their beliefs.

"Who's the moderator of the panel?" Conner asked, sitting back in his chair, his hands resting on the dark blue tablecloth.

"That would be me," I answered, glancing at my phone where it sat next to my water bottle. Another two minutes before I had to play 'moderator' and run the panel.

My eyes drifted around the room, and I frowned. Sitting in the front row was Dr. Hoel. He noticed me watching him and he gave me a slight knowing smile, his eyes twinkling.

Damn! I found him distracting and had to tear my gaze away. I'd have to remember to look everywhere in the room except at him or else I'd never be able to concentrate.

"Time for us to get started." I informed my fellow authors, before projecting my voice to be heard over the scattered conversations. "If someone would close the door, we're going to begin." There's always someone who will close them and shut out the noise. "Let's have our panelists introduce themselves."

The fifty minutes flew by. Luckily no one proved to be overly talkative, and we had a great discussion, with audience participation, about our favorite dragon novels and why. Yes, believe it or not, our vampire writer had the flying reptiles in his stories.

At the end we made our final comments, the staff member who had snuck in, opened the door. I gathered up my water bottle and wolf, putting them back in my Celtic dragon bag. Pulling it and my purse over my shoulder I headed out.

"Very good panel," Dr. Hoel complimented when I reached the main area filled with fans chatting with each other.

"Thank you." Why did he keep looking at me with those golden-brown eyes? I had a hard time looking away. "Glad you enjoyed it."

"Are all the panels that entertaining?"

"Depends on the subject matter and who's leading them."

"You seem very at ease."

"Did a lot of presentations in college and I've gotten used to being in front of crowds." Had taken me years to get comfortable without my voice quivering, my palms sweating, and steel tipped butterfly wings slicing my stomach.

"Would you go to dinner with me this evening?"

Wait a minute, had this accomplished and good-looking scientist just asked me to go to dinner?

"Uh." I stopped, swallowed, and tried to put together a coherent sentence. "I'm sorry what?"

He chuckled. I felt his fingers lightly touch my cheek like a kiss of winter wind. "I would like to take you to dinner."

"That's hours away." *Oh, brilliant.*

"Agreed." He took a step closer, and I could feel his magnetism. "You intrigue me."

Intrigue. Not a word I'd ever heard a man use when talking to a woman, particularly one who had offered to take me to dinner. Might be a nice change since I always packed a cooler full of food, currently in the back seat of my car, to save money.

"Why do I intrigue you?" I couldn't help but ask.

Sadness briefly flashed across his face. No clear idea why. I sensed his feeling as well and tried to shove my shield into place. If I didn't, I wouldn't survive the weekend. Too many crazy and excited emotions flying about.

I knew what it felt like to be sad. I certainly suffered enough of it during my life and wondered if my eyes reflected my feelings.

He continued, "It's been a long time since I took an interest in a woman."

Strange thing to say, enough to make me want to get to know him better or else run to the mountains and hide in a cave, preferably one without a wild bear or a mountain lion. "Okay," I heard myself agree.

He smiled. "Thank you."

"What time?" I knew I had some free time between five and seven. I had to be back at seven for the mass signing. Both of my publishers would be there and I was expected to attend.

"I see from the program you are free after five is that correct?" I nodded. He smiled and continued. "Why don't we meet at five-thirty?"

"That works. Bottom of stairs near the water containers?" The hotel put out containers of water filled with various fruits for their guests to drink.

"I will see you then, Ms. Landon." He darted off and ducked into the next room. The one assigned for all the Science panels and experts.

I had a date. Or at least I hoped I did.

~ * ~

What did I just do? Bertram asked himself as he took his place with the other science experts. He knew the danger he might be putting her in and had asked her to dinner anyway. His interest in Cira Landon had nothing do with tasting her.

He gave a slight smile knowing the theme he pondered had been used in more popular vampire novels, TV shows and films than he cared to remember. Did not make them any less true. How many friends had he lost due to a pretty face or a winning smile? He deeply regretted his actions in regard to his once good friend Lionel Martelli and his hunter woman.

Turning his thoughts away from painful memories, he tried to concentrate on the questions being asked. Still, his long past haunted him, filled with beheadings, stakes jabbed through a still beating heart and bodies scorched beyond recognition.

"Dr. Hoel?"

With a jerk, Bertram realized he had been brooding instead of paying attention. "I'm sorry, what was the question again?"

Earned him some chuckles from the other panelists and the audience.

"We've all been there," Tom quietly shared from his place next to Bertram.

The moderator repeated the question and Bertram answered it, forcing his mind away from his unease about taking Cira out to dinner. She and his past distracted him. He wanted to make a good impression with his fellow panelists and the audience. He had other convention invitations waiting at home for his response. He'd chosen this one as a trial run.

Before he knew it the panel had concluded and he hurried out the door, hoping no one wanted to speak with him. Darting around the blue box he took the three stairs leading up to the lobby level and on to the elevators.

Making good his escape, he closed the door to his hotel room, and sat down at the desk where he set up his laptop. Unlike many of the older vampires, he rather liked electronics, particularly ones allowing him to send messages to his friends. Much more convenient than writing letters, having them delivered by horseback, taking days or weeks before he received a response.

He scratched his chin on discovering an email from Isaac Rosen. His long-time friend currently lived in Boston and had since before the revolutionary war. Bertram remembered the days when the city had been a series of islands until many areas and the Back Bay had been filled in. Today, the neighborhood featured lovely brick homes and proved to be a desirable place to live.

With a click he opened his friend's email.

Hello Bertram, I hope your first foray into the world of Science Fiction proves fruitful. Don't forget to feed yourself well and if a lovely lady should catch your eye, although the odds of that happening might be slim from what I've seen of the local crowd, don't hesitate to indulge yourself. You've spent too much time alone.

A warning has been passed my way and I am forwarding it on to you. Lionel Martelli is headed for Denver and may be there already.

He recently won the challenge for mob leadership in the despicable city of crime. Not sure if you knew of it. Reports I received placed a high body count on known former members.

Given Martelli's nature and love for running trafficking rings, I suspect he's headed west to arrange more. He no doubt has waiting orders to fill for rare blood types, slaves and other activities he uses to make a profit.

I hear he pirates information from blood banks, hospitals and doctor's offices plus bribes employments offices and staffing services. Facts I'm sure you are well aware of.

A growl escaped Bertram's lips. He knew all about Martelli's trafficking rings. Slaves, prostitutes, domestic labor for his human clients. For his private vampire accounts rare blood types, women for harems or victims for those who enjoyed the thrill of killing. The Italian mobster had amassed a fortune over the past one hundred fifty plus years plying his trade.

Several government agencies had tried to catch him. They'd all failed. Rumors said he'd bribed officials.

Even he'd tried to stop his one-time friend. He hadn't succeeded. His efforts had increased the bitterness between them, forcing them to continue on their separate paths.

He pushed the memories aside and read the rest of the message.

I'm aware of the bad blood between the two of you and have no doubt Martelli will target you. Perhaps one day you will share the full details on what happened so I may understand the nature of the conflict. My talents include diplomacy, needed as an Elder, although I doubt the mobster will listen to anything other than brute force from what I understand of his nature.

Bertram knew what his friend meant. Martelli had come over from the old country and had immediately begun amassing power and money. First by being an enforcer for the then city boss and later moving up the ranks to become the leader himself, as he'd just learned.

My wife Racheal sends her well wishes along with her typical scolding about finding yourself a mate. She is a dear and I love her more every day. It is rare a human marriage will last fifty years, let alone over two hundred as we have shared as vampires.

Should you be so fortunate, do not let her escape.

Your old friend,

Isaac Rosen

"I doubt I will be as fortunate as you," he murmured, his eyes scanning through the emails. No others from friends and several he planned to delete.

His business email he'd check on Monday after the convention. At this hour, his university staff would have gone home and wouldn't be back in the office until Monday.

Noticing the time, he quickly shut down the program and readied himself to meet the lovely Cira Landon. With any luck his infatuation with the woman would fade by the time the convention ended and he would be able to continue his life much as he always had.

He left his room and found Cira waiting for him in the designated spot. Her tentative shy smile gave him a clear indication it might not be so easy to escape her charms. Not to mention the soothing scents of vanilla and apple mixed with the enticing salty copper of her rushing blood.

"How has your day gone?" he asked, giving her his most charming smile.

"Hectic between my panels and having to spend time in the dealer's room doing PR work for my books at both my publisher's tables."

"I haven't visited the dealer's room yet." He had all he needed or wanted. From experience, he knew research always proved useful to know what others sought to buy and would help him at future conventions.

"It's not huge like other local conventions. Normally, I don't attend those."

"Why not?" He found his curiosity growing.

"Uh mmm, that's sort of hard to explain. When I try to, they just say I have a fear of crowds."

Her answer made him curious. "I take it that's not the case?"

"Like I said, hard to explain to someone who doesn't really understand. Where are we going?"

She'd done a good job at changing the subject. He'd play along. "Where would you like to go?"

"There's a place close by that always serves breakfast."

"Sounds delightful." He offered his arm. "If you'll lead the way?"

~ * ~

During dinner I noticed Dr. Hoel ate his steak nearly rare. My ex-brother-in-law had his prepared the same way, so I didn't really think much about his preference. He completely ignored his mashed potatoes and whatever the lumpy yellow vegetable might be, which didn't even look good to me.

I had a spinach and olive omelet with some toast and a lovely cup of tea, the one thing the two of us both seemed to enjoy. He had two cups with lots of sugar and cream. I drink mine plain, though on occasion I'd add lemon.

"How long have you lived here?" He pushed his plate away and sipped his tea.

"A number of years." I felt stuffed. "I moved here during an economic downtime and had always intended to leave. Then I met my now ex-husband and well, you know how it goes."

He frowned, his eyes seeming to glow. Probably just a reflection of the overhead light. "Not in the same way."

"You ever marry?" I couldn't imagine a man with his looks not catching some woman's eye.

"A long time ago," he replied quietly. I almost didn't hear him over the loud conversations around us.

I hadn't chosen a fancy place, just an old-fashioned diner with silver and red everywhere. The waitstaff dressed like the 1950s and the air filled with the smell of grilled burgers, onions and apple pie.

"What happened?" I really hoped he hadn't suffered the same fate I had.

"She died." He put down his cup on the white and red checked tabletop.

"I'm sorry," I said quietly, feeling terrible for asking.

"No reason for you to be. I've mourned her loss."

Yet you're still alone, I commented to myself, much as I would have loved to have asked more questions. His expression and tone seemed to indicate it was an off-limits subject, so I floundered around trying to think of a topic we could talk about.

"Dr. Bertram Hoel!" an accented voice greeted. I glanced in the direction it had come, not failing to notice the flash of anger across the scientist's face.

"Hello, Mr. Martelli," my date returned.

Wait a minute. When I had I decided he was my date?

"I'm hurt," the pepper haired man pouted making his craggy face more prominent. He looked sharp in his probably tailor-made suit, with his white shirt and deep red tie. "You used to call me Lionel."

"A long time ago."

I caught the implied 'before', meaning some event they both knew about and wouldn't speak of publicly. Not to mention the emotions running between the two men. Anger being the strongest and almost overpowering. Clearing my throat, I used the distraction to try and get my shield back in place. I still hadn't learned how to keep it up all the time.

"And who is this lovely creature?" His predatory chocolate-brown eyes fixed on me. I wanted to run.

I suspect if he could have avoided it, Dr. Hoel would not have introduced me. He took a deep breath before he replied. "This is Cira Landon. She consented to have dinner with me."

"Did she now?" Martelli mused. "Willingly?"

Dr. Hoel frowned. "Of course."

"You have more courage than I gave you credit for." The Italian chuckled.

I cringed.

"I'll leave you to your meal." He cast a significant glance from Dr. Hoel to me and back again. "If you are around for the next few days, I would enjoy catching up."

"I have appointments scheduled."

Nice dodge, I silently complimented him.

"I'm sure you do." Martelli turned and gave me a calculated smile. "Have a pleasant evening, Miss Landon." His gaze returned to my companion. "We'll talk later." His tone sounded like a veiled threat.

He strolled away and I shuddered. "I don't like him."

"Nor do I." He motioned for the check. "I apologize for his bad manners."

"He was just…creepy." The word I really wanted to use—terrifying.

"You aren't wrong." He paid for dinner and stayed almost unnaturally close to me for the short walk back to the hotel.

"Thank you for dinner," I said after he safely delivered me to the second floor while set up for the mass signing bustled around me. Both my publishers had claimed a corner spot leaving some chairs open between them for their authors.

"You're welcome." His eyes glanced over at the activity. "How do you happen to have two publishers here?"

I giggled. A bad habit when I get nervous. "My small press publisher always comes. The other one I convinced to attend when they realized several authors who have written for them are local."

"That's why the empty chairs." At least he'd figured it out and I didn't have to explain it to him. With brilliant people, it's difficult to know. Their science is second nature. How to drive a car, for example, completely bewilders them.

"Exactly." *Did this guy have any idea the affect he had on me?* I hadn't been this attracted to a man since I'd first met my ex. Considering how my marriage had worked out, I had no intention of making the same mistake twice nor making the assumption he had any interest in me past going out to dinner.

"Are you staying at the hotel or returning home?" he asked me, his eyes focusing on me.

I blinked, caught off guard by his question. "Commuting. I have two cats at home wondering why their dinner is late."

He released a full laugh. I heard its echo bounce off the high ceiling. "You make them sound almost human."

"You ever lived with a cat?" He shook his head. "As they say, dogs answer to their masters, but cats are the master." I did a curtsey. "I am their humble servant."

"I believe the law says they are property and you're their owner."

"Lawyers know nothing about cats."

He smiled and man, how I would love to wake up with him every morning. "No doubt they need to be educated." His golden-brown eyes sparkled.

"No doubt," I agreed. "I need to get over there." I motioned to the tables set up in a square U shape. On the other side of the stairs was the hotel restaurant and bar.

"Of course." How in the world had he gotten a hold of my hand? I noticed his cool fingers. "Do you mind if I walk you to your car?"

"You don't really need to. It's not like I haven't done this many times on my own."

"I have no doubt you are a capable independent woman. One of the things I admire about you." His lips brushed my hand causing me to shiver. "I will rest easier knowing you left here safely."

"After the signing I'd planned on touring the art show." I waited to see how he'd respond.

"I'm a night owl," he replied.

~ * ~

Bertram could watch Cira from a table across the room. The bar stood behind him, a five-foot wooden wall separating it from the rest of the area. Clanking noises sounded and voices rose and fell. He caught scents of fish, meat, and beer. After years of practice he'd learned to tune them out.

Cira smiled as a woman stood before her, shyly asking for her books to be signed. She chatted with her fan and then introduced her to the author sitting next to her, pointing to one of the novels in the stack.

His sharp ears picked up the conversation. "That book there," Cira said, "was written by Bertha. I'm sure she'd love to sign it for you."

"I had no idea," the fan breathed, handing the book to other novelist. "If you wouldn't mind."

"I'd love to," Bertha responded, picking up her pen. She wore a warm colored dress and had long dark hair she'd pinned back. He didn't miss the protective man standing nearby nor the gold bands on both his and her fingers. "Would you like it personalized or just signed?"

"Personalized please. My name is Frances."

The other author signed the book. "I hope you enjoy it."

"I've already read it and I did." Frances moved away.

For the next hour the conversations pretty much ran the same and he half listened. He sipped the wine he'd ordered, one of the few beverages he still enjoyed. From the delicate flavor he'd bet it came from the vineyard of a dear friend who lived in California.

Finally the mass signing ended and Cira said her goodbyes to her publishers and various writer friends. He rose and re-joined her, not missing the curious looks she received.

"Everyone, this is our Science Guest of honor, Dr. Bertram Hoel." She quickly introduced her friend Bertha Hansen and her husband Kurt Ross. They had the look of a couple who had been married for a long time. Her small press publisher, Karyn Arnold, still sat at the table. She was a woman with a warm smile and also Heather Lowry, who ran events for Haley House, a branch for some sort of women's channel only available via subscription.

"My pleasure," he assured them all. "Cira, I seem to recall you wanted to tour the art show."

"I do yes." She waved at her friends. "See you tomorrow."

He took her hand and walked the short distance to the room filled with print and 3-D art. She checked her bags at the front.

Bertram didn't miss her uneasy glance in the direction of a tall silver haired man standing and talking to a shorter one with long gray hair. Both wore jeans and long-sleeved shirts.

"My ex, Paul," she explained, moving down between the aisles. "I have no desire to talk to him."

"Have you told him this?"

"No. He's got this thing about being Mr. Popular and I refuse to play the role of the horrible ex-wife, even though he deserves it."

"Interesting choice." Briefly his mind flashed to his wife's funeral. All the well-meaning friends who had tried to comfort him. He'd lost her and their son, during childbirth. Not an uncommon way for a woman to die before the advent of modern medicine. While he carried the memory, his sorrow had vanished long ago.

"Let's just say I didn't think our mutual friends needed to choose sides." She stopped to admire a picture with dinosaurs. "I really like this painting."

The price seemed high to him although he had to admit it had a likable quality.

She glanced at him. "The artist is a big name and does commission pieces for the folks at NASA."

"Explains his pricing." He cocked his head to one side. "Would you like to have it?"

"I already live in an art gallery and am out of wall space. Besides," she leaned against him, whether intentional or not, he wasn't certain. "Just because I want something doesn't mean I should own it."

Being used to buying whatever he wanted, he found her idea interesting, not to mention her scent proved distracting. His hunger stirred and he clamped his control into place. "I had never thought of that."

"Who's this?" The man she'd identified as her ex-husband stood blocking the aisle, making it difficult to pass due to the panels constructed to display art being close together.

With a casual eye he took in the man who had once been married to Cira. Very tall, broad, not really in shape if his protruding abdomen was any indication and completely at home in his casual attire.

"He's one of the con's guests of honor," Cira explained. "As if anyone I want to spend time with is any of your business." He heard the sharpness in her tone.

Her ex, Paul, glared at her and turned angry brown eyes at him. "You don't want anything to do with her."

"I'll be the judge of that," Bertram returned, knowing how to handle jealous men. His hand moved to the small of her back. "I suggest you allow us to pass as the convention has rules against harassment."

A momentary startled look passed over the man's face, the wrinkles around his eyes pronounced. "Whatever." He stomped off.

"Lucky, he didn't lose his temper. He's uncontrollable when he does." He could feel her trembling.

"I could have handled him." He knew his supernatural strength gave him the advantage. If he'd had to, he would have used it. Cira brought out his protective nature.

Cira sighed. "We should go."

"Whatever you wish." His anger surfaced, vowing he would find a way to deal with her ex for ending their pleasant evening.

~ * ~

My ex had pretty much ruined my evening. I felt Dr. Hoel's arm around me as he walked me out to the parking garage. I always made a point of finding a spot on the lowest level, making it easier to locate my car, not to mention less walking distance to the hotel back door entrance.

"Are you all right?" Dr. Hoel sounded concerned. I'd blocked out his intensely protective feelings as they were overwhelming.

"I will be," I answered.

"Do you mind me asking what your husband did to you?"

We reached my car. I dumped my purse and tote bag inside on the blue seat, keeping the keys in my hand. "He spent most of our marriage telling me what a disappointment I was to him and telling me 'if only you'd done this' in a whiny little boy voice." I crossed my arms over my chest. "His temper tantrums made him dangerous and I never knew if…" Ashamed I glanced at the stained concrete floor. "I'd reached the point I honestly thought he'd was going to kill me."

"There was no one you could have gone to?" I picked up his

tenderness in both his voice and emotions.

"You don't understand." Many people didn't unless they'd lived through it. "I'd reached a point I was too scared of what he'd do if I left him or if I stayed. It's...paralyzing." I took a deep breath trying to calm my pounding heart. "The day he walked out the door freed me."

"This convention is your only contact with him." More of a statement than a question. Probably his scientific brain clicking in analyzing the situation.

"Yes. I'm not important to him anymore."

"You are to me." The next thing I knew Dr. Hoel had his arms around me. I hadn't been held by a man for a number of years and had no idea how to react. "Am I making you uncomfortable?"

"You surprised me." I dared to return the embrace. After all, I gave all my friends hugs.

"With your permission, I'd like to kiss you goodnight."

"What a pretty scene." I tensed, recognizing the voice of the man who had interrupted our dinner.

Dr. Hoel turned, keeping himself between me and Martelli. "Why are you here?"

"I could tell from her sweet scent she has a rare blood type." The creepy scary man advanced, his chocolate eyes looking at me like I was the main dish on the menu.

Every instinct told me run. I knew better. With predators, you stand your ground and fight back if they attack. Make them think you're not worth it and they'd hopefully give up.

"Leave her be," Dr. Hoel warned.

"And allow you the only taste?" The Italian grinned. "I think not."

Taste? What did that mean?

How in the world he got past Dr. Hoel and grabbed my arm I have no idea. I felt a sharp pain piercing my flesh and I screamed, beating his back with my other hand. Warmth oozed down and I saw red splashing on the concrete.

A howl like I've never heard before sounded and a confusing fight I could barely follow ensued. I felt my body slide down the side of my light blue car, blood continuing to flow out of my wrist. My head got fuzzy and I think maybe I passed out.

"Cira?" I heard Dr. Hoel call to me from what seemed a long distance. "Cira!"

My eyes fluttered open. His light red hair seemed mussed, and I think he had dripping cuts on his face. He knelt beside me and grabbed my bleeding arm. "This is going to hurt. I'm sorry."

For the second time teeth sank into me. I tried to pull away, but his other arm kept me from moving. Lips touched my wound, a sucking sensation seeming like it took an eternity, and then something wet.

"That should stop the bleeding."

"What?" I couldn't move. My limbs hung limp and heavy. One word cost me more energy than I would have thought possible.

"He tried to drain you."

My muddled mind couldn't make sense of what had happened. Stuff like this only happened in the movies or books not in real life. *Right?*

"Where?" I wanted to ask where Martelli went.

"He's gone." His slightly warmer fingers touched my throat. "I need to get you to a clinic."

My vision blurred and all I wanted to do was close my eyes and sleep.

"Don't go to sleep!" he ordered.

I heard the car door open.

"Keys," I muttered.

"I have them," Dr. Hoel assured me.

I had the sensation of being lifted up and then nothing at all.

~ * ~

Bertram paced outside the metal door waiting for Dr. Malik to give him an update. In every city, Denver being no exception, the vampire kingdom kept an emergency clinic for cases like Cira's. A safe place where a victim could be brought and treated with no questions asked.

The door opened and Dr. Malik exited. The dark-skinned man wore a white lab coat and held a laptop in his hands. He gave Bertram a warm smile. "You got her here in time."

Feeling wobbly on his feet, he reached out and placed his hand against the peach-colored wall. Whether from relief or his own need for blood, he wasn't sure.

"Looks like you could use some blood yourself." The doctor motioned to one of the nurses. "Take Dr. Hoel to the feeding station."

He allowed himself to be led down the narrow hall into another room with colorful couches and pale green walls.

"Got into a fight, did you?" the nurse, a beefy man asked. He looked rather silly in cartoon scrubs.

"Without feeding." A bad mistake on his part and the first lesson Isaac had taught him. *Never* engage in a fight unless at full strength.

"Fresh or canned?"

"Fresh," he answered, knowing he'd heal faster.

"Be right back."

Slowly he sank onto a brown upholstered couch, his head in his hands. Knowledge of having to take Cira's blood to stop the bleeding haunted him. His tongue touched his teeth, the memory of her vanilla apple sweetness filling his mind making him want to charge into her room and drain every precious drop.

A weight settled next to him. "Do you want to know her name?" the male nurse asked.

He shook his head. Better if he didn't.

"She's one of our regulars so play nice." He listened to the retreating footsteps and didn't even look at the slightly sour smelling woman beside him. Probably a street person who donated either for a sum of money or a fresh meal and would not be missed if they vanished. He knew on occasion it happened.

With ease he bit into her arm, taking only what he need-ed to heal his body, and sealing the wound with his saliva. In a few hours, the injury would disappear. He felt her drop back and left the room knowing the nurses would take care of her.

Back outside Cira's room he waited for permission to check on her. His mixed thoughts and feelings for her con-fused him. He suddenly understood Isaac's words about deny-ing himself the pleasures he'd avoided since his wife's death. Every nerve in his body cried out for her and he flexed his fingers trying to ease the sensation.

Dr. Malik exited another room and joined Bertram. "You can see her. She's going to be a bit woozy and probably not too coherent. It would be best if you took her home."

He'd probably find her home address on her car registration. No doubt he could find the location by using his phone's GPS.

"How much blood did she need?" He almost dreaded the answer.

"More than normal." A brief silence and Malik spoke again. "Did you taste her?"

"Had too, the best way to stop the bleeding." He had to drink enough of her blood so his body could produce the needed enzymes to seal the wound.

"A good move." The dark-skinned man looked at him curiously. "I understand you made the discovery on how it works."

One of his lesser-known discoveries and only of use in their vampire world. He nodded.

"You said I should take her home." He shook himself trying to clear his bleak thoughts.

"Make sure she drinks plenty of orange juice and eats." He handed Bertram a list. "These foods would be best."

He folded the list and tucked it into his pants pocket. "She has to appear at the local convention tomorrow."

"Ah, yes, I'd heard you were in town for it." His teeth flashed white when he smiled. "I have several friends who will be attending tomorrow."

"Are you a fan?"

"I enjoy gaming and will be by tomorrow evening to play."

He knew where the gaming room was. Maybe he'd drop in and say hello. Or maybe not. Even socializing between vampires could tip off observant humans.

Malik pushed the door open. "Go sit with her. In about thirty minutes you can take her home."

"Thank you."

"It's what I do." Another vampire rushed in carrying a child. The doctor left to aid her.

Taking a seat next to Cira, he took her warm hand, lightly kissing it.

A smile touched her thin lips. "Hi."

"How are you feeling?" He averted his eyes from the now

empty bag of the life-giving fluid they'd had to pump into her.

"Other than now I know how a victim of a vampire feels?" She coughed. "My throat is dry."

A bottle of water rested on the stand. He got it for her and supported her as she took a few swallows. Settling her back against the white pillows, he sat back down. She still looked pale.

"They're letting you go home soon."

"No overnight stay for a brush with death?"

"It's only a clinic."

"Oh." She closed her eyes. Her breathing slowed into a regular rhythm.

"This would be the best time to move her," Malik said from inside the door. "She won't feel any discomfort."

She might not, but he would.

Chapter 2
The Con Saturday

There's nothing like waking up and discovering a half-naked man in your bed.

Turning on my side I dared to look at Dr. Bertram Hoel. His bare chest had brownish hair, rather thick almost as if he were part wolf. Made me wonder if he could turn into one like many of the stories said vampires could.

I remembered how it had felt to be held by his muscular arms and I got the hint his legs might be the same. Couldn't quite tell because a blanket covered the lower half and I hoped he hadn't slept nude.

My eyes drifted to the alarm clock. Six a.m. My alarm would go off in another hour. Luckily my first panel didn't start until eleven. Plenty of time to get up and around. For now, I just wanted to rest.

I pulled the blue blanket up over my shoulders and jumped when I felt a hand securing it around me.

"You need to keep warm."

"You put me to bed?" I felt my face get hot at the thought of him seeing me without my clothes, although I could feel a gown over my body.

"I'm not unfamiliar with a woman's body." He sounded amused as if he'd read my mind. "I stayed to take care of you."

"Thanks." My face must be bright red.

"Lucky for me all my panels are in the afternoon," he continued. I got the impression he might be unaware of my discomfort, and it probably was a good thing.

"We'll need to leave a little after ten for me to arrive on time." I frowned. "Where's my car?"

"In your garage."

"You know how to drive?" I'm not sure why the possibility surprised me.

"I invest in every century I live in. Makes living much more enjoyable."

"So," I hesitated unsure about what was safe to ask a vampire, although why I had a flare of jealousy I couldn't understand. "How many women have you known?"

A shadow passed over his angular face and his eyes flashed. "Only one."

His answer startled me. I would have guessed more or so the legends about vampires seemed to indicate. My face burned and meekly I asked, "Your wife?"

He nodded.

"How come?" Maybe not the best thing to ask, but I really wanted to know.

"My choice." His thumb lightly caressed my cheek. "I had other desires to pursue."

Had to give him credit, he sure knew how to avoid answering a question. "And if I asked?"

"Let us say I have more degrees than anyone living."

Fair enough, I wouldn't push. Explained his knowledge and expertise in many science disciplines and I wondered how many degrees he actually had.

My hand sneaked across the sheet and I lightly touched his chest. He gasped and grabbed my fingers. "That is dangerous."

"Dangerous how?" I teased.

"You are not strong enough." How had Bertram gotten so close to me? His arms snaked under the blankets and I found my body being held right next to his. "There will come a time when you might be."

"Might be?" My heart pounded and desire ran through my veins. I wanted him to touch me everywhere.

He kissed my forehead. "Not now. You are still too weak."

I laid my head on his chest and it took a second to realize I couldn't hear a heartbeat.

Lips nuzzled at my throat, and I groaned. Pleasant shivers ran along my arms and into my lower belly. "You tease," I accused him, my body wanting more.

He chuckled. "Just a hint." Tossing back the blankets he got out of bed. "I see you have a guest bathroom. Do you mind if I take a shower?"

Took a moment for me to catch my breath. *Good lord! The affect he had on me.*

I watched as he crossed the brown carpet. Dr. Hoel, Bertram, had a nice physique. A well-developed chest, flat stomach and a very obvious cute butt under his boxers. I'd bet he worked out, although I'm not really sure if vampires needed to.

"Fine," I finally managed, answering his question.

"Enjoying the view?" His eyes danced as he left.

I both wanted him to come back and continue his exploration as well as throw something at him for stirring up my desire and leaving me wanting.

"Ohhh!" No going back to sleep now. I crawled out of bed and headed for the shower myself, realizing as the water hit me, it could hold two people. I blushed again and tried to push the image of our bodies entwined out of my mind.

I had to be at the con in a couple of hours and I needed to get my desires under control. Time to imagine what might be later. Right now, I needed to get cleaned up and dressed. I had fans to talk to and books to sign.

~ * ~

They arrived at the convention with fifteen minutes to spare, after Cira fed her cats and made sure they got a good pet before they left. She'd had to search for a spot to park on the lower level. Together they hurried to the stairs leading down to the lobby area. She pointed to the bag he carried. "You always have an overnight bag?"

"After going to the clinic I stopped and packed it quickly. You were asleep and I figured it would be safe to leave you alone for a few minutes."

"Lucky I didn't wake up."

He didn't bother to tell her Dr. Malik had given her a mild sedative. "What time is the Haley House event this evening?" He already knew, but wanted to distract her and himself. He hadn't felt desire this strong in over two centuries.

"Seven. It's open to the public and Heather is hoping we'll have a larger turn out than last night."

Her hand trembled and he knew she'd eaten a light breakfast. "Are you all right with that?" He wanted to make certain she'd be strong enough for the event which meant a great deal to her writing success.

"Looking forward to it." She stopped at the bottom of the

stairs. "Should I feel this tired?"

"You will for a couple of days." He looked at her pale face and wondered if maybe she should have stayed home. "Make certain you drink plenty of orange juice." He pulled the list he stuffed in a side pocket of his bag. "Here's a list of foods the doctor suggested."

Cira took it with a nod, making a face. "I never eat fish and really? Liver? Ugh."

"If you get too tired come find me. You can rest in my room." He'd also make sure she ate a good meal. He'd memorized the suggestions.

Her gray eyes gave him an uncertain look. He didn't have to read her mind to know her thoughts.

"If I had wanted to take advantage of you, I would have done so last night." One look at her naked body and *all* he had desired to do was explore every inch. He'd resisted because love making should be enjoyed by both parties. He put a cotton gown on her before putting her under the covers.

Her cheeks flushed red. "You're broadcasting."

"And your dress displays every lovely curve you have." Cira wore a tight fitting long sleeved black gown, belted at the waist. Cat earrings hung at her ears and pendant of Bast rested between her breasts. He restrained his hands from exploring them. "I would suggest you hurry to your panel before I forget myself and drag you to my bed."

She gasped and he opened the door for her so she could escape. Cira hurried away from him, and he followed more slowly, intending to visit the dealer's room and possibly the art show. Although maybe he should avoid the latter as he'd be tempted to let her foolish ex-husband know exactly what he'd given up.

With a wicked smile he considered doing just that and then remembered Cira had said the man had a dangerous temper. No need to provoke a fight and cause a scene, which might endanger not just himself, but other people.

He stopped at his room dropping off his bag, before returning to the second floor. He entered the dealer's room, nodding at Karyn, and at the man he assumed was her husband, whose booth sat right by the door. She had Cira's titles prominently displayed, and several people stood looking at them.

Across from her sat a booth filled with teas. The delightful smells caught his attention, and he spent some time talking with the young woman running it. He bought two different kinds and wandered the rest of the fairly good-sized room.

He found a mix of colorful costumes hanging on racks, bearing little resemblance of what he remembered from the time period represented. Sparkling jewelry displayed on wire racks, more small publishers with stacks of books, author's tables, a local independent bookstore, gaming supplies, action figures, T-shirts and much more than he ever imagined. When he made the final turn, he found Cira seated next to Heather at the Haley House table. She sipped water and looked more tired than she had an hour ago.

"How are you feeling?" he asked her concerned, she might not have enough strength to get through the day.

She glanced at him her gray eyes slightly dull. "Like I need to take a nap."

"When's your next panel?"

"Not until four."

"Why don't I take you up to my room and you can lie down."

Her look conveyed uncertainty.

"The demonstration I'm part of starts in thirty minutes," he explained, a bit exasperated.

"That's the really long one, right?"

How long it lasted wasn't really important. "Yes. I'll check on you when I'm done."

"Okay." She grabbed her purse and dragon bag. "I'll be back in a couple hours, Heather."

Heather gave her and him a teasing look. "See you soon."

Placing his arm around her he navigated to the elevators and up to the tenth floor. He opened the door to his generic room, and she shuffled over to the bed, removing her shoes and belt.

"Can't believe how tired I am." She settled back on the outlandish flowered bedspread.

He found an extra blanket in the closet and put it over her. "Just rest. When I come back, I'll bring you some lunch."

"Okay," she mumbled as her eyes closed.

With a last worried look at Cira, he closed the door and went to his panel.

$\sim * \sim$

I'm not really sure what woke me. Maybe the strong lavender scent or the sense of someone moving around the room. I barely opened one eye to see who it was and almost screamed before I recognized Bertram.

My heart pounding I slowly sat up, needing to use the facilities.

"You're awake. I planned on letting you sleep another thirty minutes."

I glanced at the time. Two thirty. I'd been out a couple of hours. "Be right back." After taking care of business I went back into the main room. One wall had been painted a rose shade while the others a pale shade of green. The flowered bedspread had both colors in it.

Bertram had set up a plate on the desk. His laptop was plugged in and I assumed charging. I'd never heard of vampires using electronics and I'm not sure why it seemed odd. Maybe because my impressions had been formed by movies or TV shows of creepy castles and creatures who never moved beyond the century they'd lived in.

"I brought you salad with chicken." He grinned. "They're on the list."

I'd forgotten he'd given me the list after tucking it into my tote bag. "What did you do, memorize it?"

"Of course." He pulled out the chair. "If you would care to sit."

Not used to his kind of gentlemen like behavior, I let him seat me and took a bite of salad. My stomach must have woken up because I had to slow myself down so I didn't inhale my meal. He'd made me tea and it smelled delicious, a lovely mix of raspberry and vanilla.

"Good tea," I complimented.

"Bought it in the dealer's room."

Of yeah, the tea booth. They were set up across from Karyn. "I'm going to have to buy myself some."

"I would like to buy some for you, if you don't mind."

Nibbling my lip I wondered if I should allow him to. After all, he'd probably be on a plane late Sunday night or Monday and I'd probably never see him again. "Where do you live?" I ate the last bit of chicken and shoved the empty plate away.

"Boston," he answered.

"Used to live there," I shared. "What part?"

"An older section of town." He sat down on a faded jade easy chair. "Many of my friends live in Brookline."

"How long have you lived there?" I turned the office chair so I could face him.

"A long time."

"Like a hundred years? Two hundred?"

He smiled. "A little over two hundred."

"And never lived anywhere else?"

"I traveled. Explored the world. Attended various universities." He learned forward. "What about you?"

"I'm not all that interesting."

"Let me be the judge of that."

"Trust me, I'm not."

"A woman does not write the books you have without some life experience behind them."

"What makes you say that?" *Don't tell me he'd actually read them!*

"By the way you describe the places and the people. You have a rare insight."

I'd never thought of my writing that way. Normally, I'd pick a place and then fill it with characters who told a story. "Thanks."

"Have you ever written one placed in Boston?"

I nodded. "A vampire tale."

Couldn't really tell what he thought from his face, but I certainly felt his amusement. "Did you now?"

"I've always wanted to go back." No harm in saying so.

"Perhaps that can be arranged." He placed a finger against his full lips. I wondered what it would be like if he kissed me, a little upset we'd been interrupted the night before.

"I'm dreaming. I can't afford to travel." My financial reality left much to be desired.

After the convention ended I had a week of vacation before I had to go back to work. "I don't make a lot as a writer, so I have a day job with health insurance."

"You must manage your time well."

"You have no idea."

~ * ~

At three thirty, he escorted Cira out of his room and down to the second floor. Before leaving she'd put her shoes and belt back on, taking the time to smooth her hair. To him it didn't matter. She was the most beautiful woman he'd seen in a long time.

When they reached the second floor, another writer on the same panel found her and they hurried to the main level, excitedly talking about their current writing projects.

Since his next presentation started at five, he decided to simply sit and watch the various convention attendees. Some were bedecked in bright elaborate costumes and others in much simpler ones. He remembered the main masquerade started soon and no doubt many of these would grace the stage for the honor of winning a prize.

Or so he understood. He'd been educated about it after one of his panels when he'd explained he'd never attended a con before and wanted to know what went on. An adoring fan had been more than willing to tell him and share some of their experiences.

His eyes drifted to the bar and he decided a glass of wine would be nice. Making his way there, he placed his order and took a chair, frowning when he realized Lionel Martelli sat at a nearby table, two lovely young women clad in tight fitting clothing draped beside him.

When his wine arrived, he thanked the waitress and decided to face the other vampire directly. "What you doing here, Martelli?" He sat down across from the Italian.

"Enjoying the beauty," he looked from one woman to the other, "of the place."

Neither of them had badges on so they weren't part of the convention.

"Besides," Martelli continued. "You and I have unfinished business." He waved the pair away. "I have business to conduct. Go wait for me in my limo."

They pouted, giving him reproachful looks as they left. They certainly had no shame in showing off their assets.

"So," the olive-skinned man leaned across the table, "did she live or did you turn her?"

"You know we have clinics for cases like this," he returned, sipping his wine.

"She's still human then," the other mused. "I might just have to visit her."

"Leave her alone," Bertram growled. "I've marked her."

Martelli gave him a satisfied grin. "So, you got your taste. Sweet, isn't she?" He rubbed his hands together. "Perfect candidate for the black market."

"Go after her and I'll challenge you."

"With incentive like that."

His hand reached across the table and grabbed Martelli by the throat. "I'll bring you before the Elders."

"As if I'm afraid of them." Not missing his opponent's uncertain expression Bertram released him. Both of them knew Isaac Rosen was an elder and had turned Bertram.

"Go home, Martelli, and stay in your crime ridden city."

"You have no authority to order that."

"But I'm close to someone who does." Isaac thought of Bertram as a son. He had no problem exploiting their relationship if need be.

"Better keep your tasty morsel close or I'll have her taken."

"If she disappears, I'll come after you."

"Maybe it's what I want."

"You'll regret it."

~ * ~

I had no idea there would be so many people. Shaken, I took my seat at the same U-shaped table where I had sat last night, in between both publishers along with about a half dozen romance writers who also had been published by Haley House.

The sound of all those people talking was deafening as their chatter echoed off the high ceiling. I wanted to cover my ears. Not to mention wanting to run and hide. Their excitement bounced off the walls and sliced through me as if they carried a sharp blade and plunged it into my stomach.

"Here," a quiet male voice spoke softly into my ear. I hadn't heard Bertram, Dr. Hoel, come up behind me. "I convinced the bar to make this for you."

The scent of raspberry and vanilla reached my nose. I tried not to cry. His simple gesture touched me. "Thanks."

"I'll not be far away watching over you."

Sipping my tea, I felt a little better and struggled to get a hold of my shield and snap it into place. It's kind of hard to explain how that works as I've learned to reach down inside my chest and pull closed a type of invisible door over my heart. Only way I can describe the process.

Women began to line up for autographs and I put a smile on my face, meeting each adoring fan and granting them a chance to gush and tell me how much they'd enjoyed my stories. Some of them even looked over my other titles Karyn displayed not far away. From the way the pile disappeared, I'd say she made numerous sales.

The event lasted longer than expected, but we made sure everyone who came got their books signed. A group had come up from Colorado Springs, another from Fort Collins and others from various smaller communities.

Heather leaned over and said, "We have invites from conventions in Phoenix and Tucson. When they're confirmed, I'll let you know."

The idea of a romance vendor at Science Fiction cons caught me by surprise and then I shrugged. Well, maybe not such a big surprise. Most of mine had been written as SF, fantasy, or paranormal.

When the last fan left, I took a deep breath and took the last swallow of tea. Even cold it tasted good.

"How'd we do, Karyn?" I asked my small press publisher.

"Almost sold out. Good thing I have a few titles stashed for tomorrow."

Sundays are always the biggest shopping day where everyone spends their leftover money on items they've already picked out. Some of the venders also have discounts so they don't have to take as much merchandise home.

I gave Dr. Hoel a smile as he walked up to the table. "Did you really watch the entire time?"

"For the most part. I had a fascinating discussion with Tom and Pat."

"Probably over my head."

"No doubt," he good-naturedly agreed, leaning over the table to plant a cool kiss on my cheek. "How are you feeling?"

"Hungry."

"Then allow me to order you dinner."

"And just where am I supposed to eat this dinner?" I had a pretty good idea and wasn't sure how I felt about it.

"The restaurant if you wish or I can have room service deliver."

The thought of spending even five more minutes surrounded by noisy people made my fingers tremble. "Your room sounds fine."

I waved at Karyn and Heather as I joined him. "I'll see you ladies tomorrow."

Bertram offered his arm and we walked together to the elevators.

Two hours later when I arrived home, I fed my cats, who of course, wanted attention, so I spent time apologizing for the supposed neglect they'd experienced. I went up the wooden stairs of my townhome and washed up for bed before crawling under the covers. My nose detected a faint musky scent and I suspected it had come from my guest of the previous night.

Funny, I had spent a couple of years after my ex left learning to sleep alone again. Now all I wanted was the comforting presence of a man, actually a vampire, I barely knew.

Figured.

Chapter 3
The Con Sunday

Blinking, Bertram rose, not really used to being awake so early in the day. His kind weren't confined to the dark of night as they'd often been portrayed in popular culture. They could be out while the sun sat in the sky. The older vampires had a higher tolerance than the newly made, should they ever be allowed to make any again.

Taking a quick shower he reflected he had always preferred later hours even as a human. His habit had driven his wife crazy, claiming he'd wasted half the day.

He dressed and checked his appearance in the large bathroom mirror. Another myth dispelled as his reflection stared back at him.

He heard the light knock on his door and he smiled. *Ah, breakfast.* He loved ordering in. Answering it, he tipped the wait person and helped himself to their blood before sending the human back to their duties. They would not remember what happened. The food he'd give to one of the fans next door. He'd overheard them, thanks to his enhanced hearing, mention they could afford the room, but not to eat. He'd taken it upon himself to help them out.

Once on the second floor he glanced around wondering if Cira had arrived yet. With a frown, he wondered how the woman had gotten past his defenses and fostered a care he hadn't shown to anyone except his deceased wife.

A faint apple and vanilla mix reached his nose and his eyes darted to the marbled stairs. Dressed in shimmering flowing green, she stood here, her gold inlaid top accenting her breasts, despite them being completely covered.

Her hair, which he could now tell the color, a deep brown, she wore down and with colorful flowers clipped into it. His fingers remembered how it had felt and he looked away, resisting the temptation to kiss her until she begged for more.

"Who are you dressing up for?" Across the carpeted floor marched Cira's ex-husband stopping before her, leaning toward her menacingly. He wore ripped jeans, a long-sleeved checkered shirt and heavy boots.

"What are you talking about, Paul?" Her exasperated tone told him she hadn't wanted to call her ex by his name. She put her hands on her hips. "You're just jealous because another man has shown an interest." She leaned toward the other man. "What happened? Your desire to play the field not turn out the way you thought it would?"

The man's face flamed red and he balled his fists. Bertram hurried to her side, seeing the confrontation drawing the attention of many con attendees. He heard a staff member say into their phone, "We need con security on the second floor."

"I have to make an appearance at the Haley House table, so if you'll excuse me." She moved to walk past him. He reached out and grabbed her arm.

Bertram's hand closed over her ex's arm. "Let go of her," he warned very quietly.

The man glared a challenge at him. Bertram increased the pressure and finally, her ex reluctantly released her.

"I suggest," Bertram warned, "that whatever you were doing you return to it. If I see you near Cira again." He allowed his eyes to flash deep red, satisfied at the inhaled breath he heard. "There are worse things that can happen."

Backing away, Paul glanced at Cira, shock on his silver bearded face as he scuttled off to the men's room. With a chuckle of amusement, Bertram wondered how close the other had come to peeing on himself.

He turned his attention to Cira. "Are you all right?" Bertram secured his arm around her.

She nodded, shaking slightly. "Normally he's all bark."

"Not today it would seem." He hated seeing her upset.

Con security arrived, wearing masks similar to what he recognized as part of a franchise for a TV show popular in the 1960s and beyond. Karyn's husband also joined them, glancing around, as if ready for a confrontation.

"You okay?" one of them asked Cira.

"Fine." She rubbed her arm. "No harm done."

"Where'd he go?" another security person barked.

She shook her head. "Wasn't watching, sorry."

"Men's room," Bertram informed them, tightening his hold on Cira.

"Please, just leave him be," Cira begged. "If you take any action it'll just make things worse."

"You want to file a complaint against him?" the first security person asked. "We can have him banned."

"This is normally the only time of year we might run into each other. Just leave it be." She took a deep breath. "Thank you for being willing to help. He'll go back to where he volunteers and since it's Sunday, he'll be busy the rest of the day."

"You sure? We want you to feel safe."

Her publisher's husband headed toward the men's room. Bertram wondered what might happen.

"I'm sure." She turned to Bertram. "Would you mind walking me to my publisher's table?"

"It would be my pleasure." Bertram escorted Cira to a quiet corner and helped her to sit down. He could feel her trembling. "Are you sure you're all right?"

"Not what I needed today."

Cira leaned against him and every instinct he had wanted to protect her. He draped his arms around her. "How many panels do you have today?"

"Two. One in about thirty minutes and another a bit later."

"You should file a restraining order." He'd check with his attorney about it.

She shook her head. "He's never acted like this. Not publicly."

A man threatens a woman just to feel superior, or so he understood from the studies he'd read. He shook his head, not understanding how a man could treat a woman so cruelly. "You deserve better."

"Thank you." Cira pulled away. "I need to take a few minutes to get myself together."

"I have nothing until one," he told her.

"You don't have to act as my escort all day." Despite her words, her expression said otherwise.

"I don't," he agreed. "But I would like to."

Her eyes searched his face and nodded, as if she answered some unasked question. "You're not allowed in the ladies room."

He laughed. "True. But I can wait for you."

~ * ~

My ex Paul is a complete jerk and an annoying idiot. I hope his actions will get circulated all over the con and he'll be lucky if he's allowed back next year. That would suit me just fine.

I stared at my image in the mirror. Still a bit too pale after my ordeal on Friday night and I tried not to react to the memory. Not to mention the confrontation I hadn't expected. What had Bertram done to scare off my ex? Paul never frightened that easily. Honestly, I don't think I wanted to know.

Besides, today is Sunday. Last day of the con. More than likely I won't see the man, both my ex and Bertram, after today, if the latter is still considered a man since he's a vampire.

Why did the thought of not seeing Bertram again make me sad? *Come on girl, don't be silly. His only interest in you is the blood flowing in your veins. He's already had a drink.* Or so my muddled mind remembered.

With a last glance at myself, I left the ladies room and found Bertram waiting for me. He gave me a warm smile, causing his eyes to glow a pleasant golden brown. My eyes unwillingly dropped looking in a direction I shouldn't. I blushed.

"And what are thinking?" he whispered seductively in my ear.

His voice made me blush even more. "You don't want to know," I replied.

"When were you last with a man?" His fingers whispered across my face.

"Will you stop!" I think I said it a bit louder than I'd intended. My words drew unwanted attention.

"My apologies." His arm rested around my waist. "I'll endeavor to control my desire for you."

"Your…" I stopped not sure how to respond.

"Why do you find that surprising?" His face held a bewildered expression. "You are a beautiful woman."

"It's just…" how could I explain? My ex never made me feel like that. *Damn!* Would the damage done by his abuse ever get better? I was tired of walking on unexpected emotional landmines.

"What is your panel on?" His question jerked my mind back to the present.

"Paranormal romance."

"Ah. One of my favorite genres."

"You read paranormal romance?" Why would a vampire even be interested?

"I find them amusing."

"Oh." Not sure how to respond, I walked with him down the stairs and watched the current panels let out. I even allowed him to walk me to my place at the table. He took a chair at the front, giving me a smile I would want a man to give me every day.

I vaguely wondered if he'd add any comments to the discussion, knowing he probably wouldn't. After all, what vampire would really want their presence known?

~ * ~

He found the discussion on paranormal romance fascinating and of course, amusing. Lots of love starved females writing about dream lovers who did not exist. Truth was, romances between humans and vampires rarely ended well. He knew of no happy endings. Either the human got turned without permission and left their lover or they went insane inflamed with desires that could never be quenched. Many committed suicide.

Unless one considered Blood Marriages and even they were the stuff of legends, giving the couple some sort of unspecified bond. The last confirmed union had happened perhaps four hundred years ago. He knew some spouses turned the other, like Isaac and Rachel. Since they were already wed they'd already formed an emotional tie and the Elders had no need to witness their union.

Thinking of this rarely performed ceremony made Bertram uneasy and he pushed it to the back of his mind, refocusing his attention on the discussion between Cira and the other panelists.

At the conclusion of the panel, he waited until Cira packed her stuffed wolf and water, before he rose and walked with her out of the room. She seemed calmer and he hoped she didn't allow her ex to ruin the rest of her day. He wondered what had happened between Karyn's husband and Paul. He doubted he'd ever learn the outcome.

"Where to next?" he asked.

"Dealer's room. Want to do my last circuit and check with my publishers."

"You expected to sit with them today?" He couldn't imagine the need. Surely everyone who was going to buy her book had done so already.

"Busiest shopping day of the con," she reminded him. "Besides,

I want to check with Heather about other cons who have expressed an interest in having us attend."

"That is good?" He wanted to make sure.

"Oh, you bet." She flashed him a smile. "Really good. More appearances and a great opportunity to expand my reader base."

He had a great deal to learn about authors it seemed. His fingers closed on hers. "Cira."

"Yes?" She stopped to look at him. They stood close to the blue box.

"I," how did he phrase this without frightening her? "I will be in Denver for a few more days. Would you mind if I called on you?"

She smiled, her gray eyes sparkling. "That's sort of an old-fashioned way to say it."

"To say what?"

"That you'd like to spend more time with me."

With a slight bow, he said, "I have business meetings to attend and am free in the evenings."

"Lucky for you I'm on vacation this week." She put out her hand. "Don't suppose you have a cell phone?"

"I do actually." He pulled it out of his jacket's inner pocket, setting up the contact page before handing it to her. "May I do the same?"

She nodded absently and handed him her phone. After entering his number, he handed it back to her. After saving the information, she stared at his number. "I see you have a Boston area code."

"As I've already shared, I've lived there for many years."

She put the device back in her purse. "I hear there have been many changes since I lived there."

"The city has changed over the years." He remembered it growing from the busy seaport of his youth to the modern-day metropolis.

"I'll bet. Are the rats still a problem?"

"I suspect they always will be."

She giggled. "I remember walking in Kenmore square and seeing a rat run across the sidewalk in front of me and under a car."

He lowered his voice. "They're good for a snack but taste awful."

"Yuck!" Cira made a face. "I won't even ask."

"Best you do not." Placing his arm around her again they took the stairs to the second level, and he walked with her around the dealer's room as she made a few purchases before he left her in the safekeeping of her publisher.

"About time you got here," Heather grumped. "I have several who said they'll come back later to get their book signed."

"I'm here until my last panel at three."

"And we close at four. Perfect."

He'd have to make certain to walk Cira to her car. Somehow, he doubted her ex would bother her again, but Martelli no doubt hovered nearby, waiting for an excuse to abduct her.

"I will return at three to escort you," he assured Cira.

She smiled, lightly touching his hand. "I look forward to it."

He dared to lift her fingers and planted a kiss there. "As am I."

~ * ~

I have to be crazy. Why in the world am I even entertaining the idea of seeing this man—vampire—after the con is over? I feel like the heroine in a paranormal novel so caught up in love I don't care whether or not he's a blood sucking monster.

"You could do worse," Heather's voice interrupted my thoughts.

"What?" How many times had I said that over the weekend?

"Honey, he is hot." She turned her laptop so I could read the page she had pulled up. "Not to mention one of the most eligible Boston bachelors and evidently rich too."

"Heather, you are shameless."

"I'm going to check out any man who takes an interest in one of my star authors."

"Oh? I'm now one of your star authors?"

"Word is spreading." She pulled her laptop away when I took no interest in reading the article she'd found. "We've gotten queries from about a dozen conventions and couple of writer's conferences." She grinned. "I released a couple of videos on social media."

"Thanks for telling me." Should have remembered Heather did all the social media campaigns.

She made a motion like brushing my comment aside. "It's good for business and good for you. Don't complain."

"Yes, mom," I mumbled.

"Smile. Potential customer."

I gave the woman looking at the titles a smile. "Hi."

"Hi," she answered. "I was at your reading. How many titles do you have out?"

"Two with Haley House and several others with Karyn there." I pointed to the corner booth. Her husband, Steven, gave her a bag and I assumed he'd brought her lunch.

"I'm going to buy them all and have you sign them."

"It would be my pleasure."

I watched as she went to Karyn, bought all my books and then came back and bought the rest. The next fifteen minutes I spent signing them and chatting pleasantly with her. She moved on, her canvas bag full, but I'd bet it would be even more so when she left.

"You see." Heather looked very proud of herself.

"Not arguing." In fact, my success made me very happy.

The next couple of hours ebbed and flowed with being busy or not, depending on what panels fans planned on attending. I talked with Heather who answered numerous emails. She'd mastered multi-tasking. Karyn wanted to know when I'd send her another book.

When two forty-five rolled around, I took a drink of water and got ready to leave.

"I'll email you your itinerary," Heather told me. "You should check with Karyn to see if she'd be willing to send along some of your other titles."

"How many cons have you confirmed?"

"I'll let you know." She grinned. "You are going to be very busy next year," she promised.

"Nice to hear. Please make sure I have time to write."

"Just bring along your laptop. You can write in your hotel room."

"Right." Heather had no idea how my creative process worked. Of course, I'd been writing long enough to be able to write no matter what my mood or location. No need for my 'muse' to inspire me. Butt in chair. That worked well for me.

I stopped to say bye to Karyn and let her know what Heather had cooked up. Promised her it was good thing and I'd be touch with the details. Our visit took longer than expected and I found myself having to hurry before my final panel when Dr. Hoel appeared at my side.

"Sorry I'm late," he apologized.

"It's fine. I'm running late."

"Then let us hurry." He followed me down to the main floor.

"I'm leaving when this is done," I informed Bertram.

"I will walk you to your car."

"You don't—"

"Yes, I do." His tone brooked not room for argument. I gave up and nodded.

The time passed quickly or seemed to. On Sunday attendance is sparse, but we had a great time discussing the ups and downs of adding dinosaurs to a story. Afterward, Bertram walked with me out to the garage, his arm around my waist.

"Sunlight doesn't bother you?"

He shook his head. "Not normally."

"So vampires only being able to exist at night is what, a myth?"

"For the most part."

"You are not real forthcoming with information."

"It is better for humans to believe the mythos they created rather than to have their illusions shattered."

"That sounds sort of condescending."

"Perhaps it is."

We stopped by my car. The garage had emptied out and I knew only the diehards would stay until the very end for the closing ceremony, which should start in a few minutes. Then would come tear down, packing everything away until next year. For many, it would be a late night.

His cool fingers lightly touched my cheek, slowly descending along my neck and arm. It felt sensual and I couldn't be sure if Bertram intended his caress to be or not. "Please stop."

"You object to being touched?" he breathed, moving closer and pulling me to him. I mean, I really should have objected, yet again, I seemed to be acting like those silly lovesick heroines so popular in romances even my own.

"No," I answered his question. "You know I really hate ties."

"Excuse me?" He blinked. Startled, I'd bet.

"Yeah." I loosened it, took it off, and handed it to him. "Put that in your pocket." My fingers undid a couple of buttons. Funny how one little move makes a man, or vampire, a bit more sexy. Or maybe it's my fascination with pirate movies and those lovely open shirts they wore. "You want to please me, don't wear one again unless the occasion calls for it."

"I see." He chuckled. "Now, where were we?"

"I'm not sure," I answered, unsure exactly what he had in

mind.

"I am."

His lips touched mine and he kissed me. I expected it to be filled with passion. Instead, it was tentative, tender and sweet. Still, it made my heart race and I wanted to drag him home into my bed.

"Good night, my dear one." He released me, opening my car door. "I'll call you tomorrow."

"Night." I crawled in and backed up, feeling like I had left a piece of me behind. When I glanced in the rearview mirror, Bertram had vanished.

Driving out of the parking garage, I wondered if it mattered whether or not he called me. I knew it did. He'd taught me I was still a desirable woman, something I hadn't felt for a long, long time. Not even when I'd been married.

Chapter 4

Monday after the Con

"Your ex-wife may be in danger or not," Jake Sutter said as he sat across the gray marbled tabletop. On the other side the silver-haired man who had contacted him fumed. For the past thirty minutes he'd listened to the sob story about how the thief, Dr. Bertram Hoel, a vampire known to the hunters, had stolen his ex-wife.

Jake rubbed his hand on his jeans, trying to alleviate the tension he felt oozing off the guy. He'd broken the nervous habit of running his fingers through his light brown hair.

"So how do I help her?" The man sipped his coffee, his brown eyes drifting around the diner. The way he dressed gave him away as a blue-collar worker. He wore a brown sweater with the white collar of his shirt peeking out with grease under his nails and streaking his tan pants.

"Does she really want your help?" Jake sat back, hearing the seat squeak. He suspected the contact hadn't really come from any concern for the woman's well-being. He'd met many jealous men with similar agendas. "You know, his fascination with her may have only been during the convention. He's known for that." Not actually. Dr. Hoel rarely took an interest in the opposite sex and he wondered why the vamp had with the man's ex-wife.

Jake looked the other squarely in the eyes. "Just a sweet taste, getting their hopes up, only to toss them aside for the next delicious morsel." He gave a hint of the truth without revealing what he knew.

"You make him sound…"

"Like a connoisseur?" Jake shook his head; glad he'd worn his favorite sweatshirt. The place had a decided chill despite the greasy burger smells drifting from the grill. "Make no mistake, Dr. Hoel might be dangerous. If he is." He finished his coffee. "Do yourself a favor, stay out of it. Leave it to the experts."

"Like you?"

"Yeah, like me. We've been waiting to find this one." He had to make it sound good.

"So, you don't want my help."

"You've told us all we need to know. You're sure he's still at the hotel?"

"Yeah, he's going to be there for the rest of the week. Not leaving until Saturday."

"How'd you find out?" The answer would tell Jake many things about his 'informant'.

"Overheard the hotel staff talking."

"What made you suspicious and how'd you find us?" Jake had gotten good at asking questions to get the information they needed.

"His eyes glowed red. Seen enough movies to know what it meant." He laughed harshly. "You can find out anything you want on the Internet."

So, the man had found their site. Good. It's how they kept track of potential troublemakers, like the guy on the other side of the table.

"Thanks for the information." Jake put a bill on the table to pay for their coffees and leave the waitress a good-sized tip. "We'll update you."

"I want to help."

"No." Jake had to be firm. The man had no idea how dangerous vamps were. He'd get himself killed and probably a number of innocents. "Go home. Let us handle this."

"But," he began, his face flushed.

"I said no." His tone allowed no argument. "We know how to contact you."

"But what if he—"

"As I said, he may only have been interested for the duration of the convention. I doubt he'll contact her again. They rarely do."

The man narrowed his eyes. "You can't be sure. I saw the way he looked at her."

Jake dared to play his next card. "I think you're upset another man paid attention to her for reasons that have nothing to do with you caring about her."

"How dare you!" he growled rising to his feet.

"Go home," Jake repeated. "We're pros and we'll handle this." He got up to leave. "And don't follow me." He pulled on his brown jacket.

Leaving the diner, he got into his jeep and watched. The other man exited, looked around and stomped to his vehicle. He gunned the engine and roared out of the parking lot, almost hitting another car as it pulled in.

Yeah, that's what he thought. He picked up his phone and called Lance Childers, the US hunter leader. "We got a tip on Dr. Bertram Hoel."

He listened to the response on the other end.

"Yeah, I'm sure and I'll be careful. Oh, and check out a Cira Landon. Local author. I'm gonna tail her. I don't think Dr. Hoel will contact her again, but just want to make sure she stays safe."

Lance said something on the other end.

"Yeah, I know. He's pretty much a loner and normally ignores the ladies. Update you later." He hung up.

With a grin, he left heading for home. He'd tail Cira for a few days and see how things developed. With any luck, the vamp wouldn't break the agreement.

~ * ~

Lucky for me, the day didn't drag since I honestly didn't expect a man as important as Dr. Bertram Hoel to call me. After all, who was I anyway? A beginning author slowly moving up in exposure and fortunate enough to land a contract with a romance publisher who happened to be waiting for my next book.

Speaking of which, I looked at my word count for the day. Not bad. My next book was more than a third completed. Well, the first draft anyway. I'd fix it during the rewrite. That's where the real writing began or so one of my editors had taught me many years ago.

Time for a stretch I decided as I got up and grinned at my two cats. They each had their own favorite napping spot, normally a chair, not the beds I had bought for them. Although today, my older female Sophie had curled up in one, my ornery and much younger male Anghel slept in my favorite chair. He'd be unhappy if I disturbed him.

My phone rang and I answered it, expecting it to be some annoying telemarketer. I glanced at the ID and realized with a start it was Dr. Bertram Hoel. Okay, so he called me. *Surprise, surprise, surprise.*

"Hi," I answered on the third ring.

"I'm not disturbing you am I?"

"Needed a break. Been a busy day."

"Working on your next novel?" I could hear the amusement in

his voice.

"Something like that."

"Yet you also work?" He sounded puzzled.

"No choice. Bills have to be paid and I like to eat." Mainly I worked to give my cats food and a place to live.

"So, while you're on vacation from your job, you are writing."

"I have a whole week, so yeah." His brief silence concerned me then I realized he may not be comfortable talking on the phone. "I didn't expect you to call until this evening." *If at all.*

"Meetings ended early," he explained. "I would very much like to take you to dinner."

"Fancy or casual?"

"What would you be more comfortable with?"

"You always do this?"

"Do what?"

"Ask a ton of questions. Most guys just make a decision and tell a woman where they're going." Like I'd really know since I hadn't dated much before or since my divorce.

"These modern times. Women should be cherished not—" he stopped. "I'm sorry. Given I'm from a different time period, I still, on occasion, have trouble adjusting to current attitudes."

I couldn't help but laugh. "It's okay. I'd prefer casual, if that's all right with you." Men liked to impress women, until they caught them. They had no idea they had to spend the rest of their lives winning the woman back every day. "I'm perfectly comfortable in my jeans."

His quiet chuckle made me smile. "Sounds like a plan. I noticed several places close to where you live."

"There are several," I agreed.

"Is an hour long enough?"

I glanced at the clock. Five thirty already? Wow. Where had the time gone? "Sure."

"Depending on traffic, I may run a little late. I'm at the hotel."

"Rush hour is pretty horrific. If you're late I won't worry." I knew the area and how bad traffic could be. Driven through DTC often enough myself.

"I'm glad you're understanding."

"You know, one day I'd love for you to share how courting a woman was different."

"Perhaps." He made no promises and I felt a little disappointed.

"As a writer, I like to know about all sorts of things." I pushed a little. The worst he could say was no.

"We'll see."

Not a no. Not a yes either. "See you when you get here and be careful. Denver drivers can be nasty and crazy."

"See you soon," he promised. Click.

I put my phone up a little miffed he hadn't let me say bye. Oh, well. Maybe he hadn't really learned phone etiquette. Saving my work, I went upstairs to change my top. Jeans on a date are fine, but not a sweatshirt.

Pulling out a sweater, I put it on and ran a comb through my hair, adding just a hint of makeup. Never been one to try to cover up how I looked. Just enhance my features.

Back downstairs I fed my cats dinner, and watched my youngest bounce off the furniture, literally, before the two wound down enough to return to the important task of washing before napping.

When the doorbell rang, they dashed up the stairs to hide. I took a deep breath and answered.

~ * ~

Bertram shuffled from one foot to the other, feeling like he had when he'd courted his wife. Luckily, he had no parents to impress and not every moment with Cira would be chaperoned. Those rituals had been done away with long ago.

As the door swung open, he stopped his nervous action and straightened, feeling almost naked without his tie. When had wearing one become so much a part of his self-image?

Cira smiled shyly at him. "Hi."

"Hello," he returned. She wore jeans and a red-orange sweater, her hair down and a touch of makeup. Her simplicity made her beautiful.

Her eyes took in his attire of jeans and long-sleeved shirt, partly unbutton. "You remembered."

"You made a point of telling me."

"I'm impressed you actually listened."

"Don't men listen?"

"Not often." She pushed open the screen door. "Come on in."

"Thank you." He entered her living room. When he'd brought

her home, he hadn't taken the time to look around. Framed fantasy prints decorated the lavender walls. The room had been set up for the comfort of one person and he wondered if she ever had company.

"Let me grab my coat." She went to the back of house and opened a door, pulling out a colorful coat.

He remembered coming in the back door. That's where her garage was.

"So where are we going?" She grabbed her purse sitting on the stairs.

"You know the area. Pick a place."

"Who's driving?"

He grinned. "Come with me."

"Okay." She locked her back door and did the same with front as they left. Cira stopped. "A limo?"

He shrugged used to traveling by limo. "The advantage of having money."

She took a step back, an uncomfortable look on her face. He took her arm. "Come, Cira. Allow me to spoil you."

"I've just never...why in the world..."

"You helped me to wake." More true than she knew. He had to control himself or else he'd drag her back into her home and make love to her.

"Say what?"

"I'll explain later," he whispered in her ear, allowing her to decide what he meant.

Cira shook herself and allowed him to lead her to the black limo. The driver got out and opened the door for them.

"I'm under dressed for a limo," she muttered.

"No more than I am," Bertram reassured her, sitting next to her. The door closed and the driver got in front.

"Where to, sir?"

"There's a restaurant I really like," Cira said. "If that's okay?"

"Anywhere you want."

After she gave the driver directions, she sat back and glared at him. "You could have warned me."

"I'm not in the habit of telling women I have money."

"Smart." She turned her head and looked out the window. "It wouldn't have mattered."

He glanced toward the front. "Just keep in mind what I have

told you before."

"I've watched enough TV shows and movies or read books." Cira moved in her seat so she could face him. "What in the world do you see in me?"

"A talented, beautiful woman who has not been told her worth." He leaned closer. "Who I am going to kiss."

"Wanna bet?" she returned, moving across the seat.

"The back has limited options. How long do you think you can avoid what I am determined to give you?" He managed to catch her and pull her next to him.

She struggled. "Let me go!" Her eyes sparkled and she gave him a smile.

The driver glanced back. Bertram supposed to make certain nothing was amiss, before his eyes concentrated on the road.

"Not until I kiss you." He slid his hand behind her head to hold her still and kissed her. Cira briefly pushed against his chest, before relaxing and kissing him back. He released her. "That wasn't so bad."

"You're a brat," she teased, giving his arm a playful slap.

"Perhaps."

They arrived at the restaurant. The driver let them out. Before he went to park the limo, Bertram asked what he wanted to eat.

"That was nice." Cira gazed at him curiously as if she'd just seen him.

"Thank you." He took her inside. Several familiar scents assaulted his nose, baked bread, meat, vegetables and sweet desserts. The décor was supposed to be French, but more of an Americanized version of it. He'd been to Paris. He knew the difference.

"Two," she told the hostess standing at the podium.

"It'll be at least a thirty-minute wait."

"No problem."

He followed her to the waiting area where they sat together in black wooden chairs. His hand took hers. "Yes, I should have told you I rented a limo."

"At least you admit it." She sighed. "I don't believe in Princess fairy tales."

"I'm not asking you to." He dared to raise her hand to his lips, brushing them against her soft skin. "Just be in this moment with me."

"I can do that. Besides," she dropped her voice. "It's not like there's a chance of any type of future for us."

Her words stung him. For he had dared, even before he'd become aware of it, of building a vision for a future with Cira.

Chapter 5
Wednesday & Watching

Jake sat in his jeep; the hood pointed in the opposite direction so he could watch Cira Landon's house. She worked on her small patio, a broom in her hands, pushing the bright orange, yellow and red leaves off onto the side. How she managed to get them to fall underneath the yellow painted fence, he didn't even want to figure out.

Earlier, she swept them off her porch and short sidewalk. Communities like this normally had a service who came in and did stuff like gardening or raking the leaves. At his small house in a more rundown part of town, he had to do all the yardwork himself. Not that he really cared as he never spent much time there.

Cira's annoying ex kept calling, asking for updates and speaking of which, the man had just called again for like the tenth time. He had to keep telling the informant to stay out of it. His inexperience could get Jake in trouble with the vampires and maybe, accidentally get some innocents killed like Cira, the woman he'd supposedly been so concerned about.

Honestly, he hadn't expected Dr. Hoel to continue seeing her. Jake had figured after the con, he'd ignore her completely, so every time he showed up to take her dinner or a trip to the zoo like he had earlie, the vampire's actions surprised Jake.

Concerned him too, although it shouldn't since the century long agreement had been kept by both sides. Still, he'd keep watch over her.

While the chances were extremely slim, he wanted to make sure Dr. Hoel didn't turn her. If he did, well, the hunters would be forced to take action.

Chapter 6
Thursday on Vacation

That weird green jeep was parked outside again. Granted it could be a new owner, several units have been for sale in our little community, but something felt off. I don't know if it's just so beat up or if it's the unusual bumper sticker saying, 'The only good vamp is a dead one'.

I shuddered and closed the gray and red striped drapes. Sophie bumped my leg and I picked her up, rubbing my hand on her soft brown fur. Her purr filled my ear and I allowed it to comfort me. Her head came up and bumped under my chin. Her sign of affection and I enjoyed it. Used to annoy my ex. Too bad he never learned to appreciate the feline's love.

Putting Sophie down, she gave me an indignant glare before jumping up on a chair and giving herself a good wash, I went into the kitchen to make some pancakes, one of my favorite breakfast meals. I'd had them for the last couple of days. One of the nice things about being on vacation, I had time to cook what I want and not warm my food up in the microwave.

Dinner the previous night had been very good. We'd gone back to my favorite place. I'd ordered the turkey meal and Bertram had a barely cooked steak. At least now I understood why. Maybe. I hadn't asked him any details about a vampire's digestive system. Didn't really want to know.

After cooking and eating, plus clean up, I had to decide what to do. The problem with our society is once you start working, you don't quite know what to do with yourself when you have time off. Maybe that's why so many don't take vacations. Plus the fact their work piles up on them like an icy road on a snowy day.

Enough about work, I reminded myself. I had a few more days left before I had to go back to my boring office job. I'd really enjoyed my time off and all the lovely writing time. My current work in progress had sped along. Wouldn't finish it during the next couple of days, but it was half finished at least.

First though, I'd walk down to the mailbox and pick up whatever junk or bills had collected. I'd skipped it yesterday. By the time we'd gotten back from the zoo, I'd been very tired. Not that I'd seen Bertram every day. He'd just shown up yesterday and off we'd gone to wander through and enjoy the animals.

Funny thing is they hadn't reacted to him, at least, not that most folks would notice. The male lion had roared at him and some of the big cats hissed. Others caring for young shielded their babies. Most had just ignored Bertram.

"I'm not their main concern," he'd told me, with a smile I was fast coming to love.

Wait a minute, love? Come on girl, get a grip. You know darn well once he goes back to Boston he's not going to give you a second thought. You're just a distraction while he's visiting. Remember that.

Yeah, right. After that heart stopping kiss last night?

Well, not heart stopping exactly. I mean, I'm still here. But wow!

The zoo. Dinner. Walking me to my door and waiting until I'd unlocked it.

"You enjoyed your day?" he'd asked, his eyes glowing golden brown. Really haven't figured out why they do that.

"Yeah," I'd answered. "Been a long time since I've been to the zoo. Just not any fun to go alone."

"You have no friends who can accompany you?" Bertram tended to phrase things a bit formal. Probably a holdover from him being over two hundred years old, a fact I should take advantage of and ask him some questions. I just never seemed to get around to it when we're together. He's so handsome not to mention all I want to do was, well, my face burned just thinking about him.

"My friends are scattered with different work schedules and life stuff."

"Unfortunate."

He hesitated, before gathering me into his arms. "I've been wanting to do this all day."

Part of me wanted him to kiss me while another part didn't. Before I could make up my mind his lips touched mine and all thoughts of resistance flew out of my head.

He'd been gentle at first, before becoming more passionate, pressing me against him, his hands wandering a bit, yet not touching me in a way a lover does.

My mouth opened and his tongue pressed inside, exploring me with a growing fervor. He pushed me against the brick wall, and I knew I needed to put an end to this before we gave my neighbors more of a show than they needed to see.

I pushed against him, forcing him back. "Enough," I'd managed.

"You're not enjoying it?" He'd sounded both puzzled and hurt.

"Not the point." The last thing I'd wanted was to stop him. "Not the place."

"I could stay."

"No." I'm not the type to invite a man I barely know into my bed. Okay, he'd shared it with me once, but not intimately. "I'm not ready."

"Far be it for me to force an unwilling woman." He'd let go. With a slight bow, he'd given me a seductive smile. "Till we meet again."

Standing there, I'd watched him leave, wondering if he'd ever come back.

Doesn't matter, I reminded myself, trying to push his hot kisses out of my head.

I glanced at the time and knew the mail had probably come. It's a short walk to the mailbox and the fresh air would help me clear my head. Grabbing both my house and mailbox keys, which I kept on a separate key chain, I headed up the slight incline, stopping to speak with various neighbors out walking their dogs.

"How's Maisy today?" I asked the older woman who owned the one-eyed dog. Her thin frame she'd covered with stretch pants and a bright yellow sweater.

"Doing fine and you?"

"Great. On vacation this week."

"Do anything special?"

"Convention and the zoo." Didn't bother to tell her about the man I had gone out with.

"Sounds good. You have a good day."

"You, too."

Reached the box, unlocked it, took the junk mail out, and headed back to the house. Maybe I'd take a nap before writing some more.

I heard a car slow and shaded my eyes from the sun. It sped up and crashed into the back of the lurking jeep, smashing the bumper sticker. The guy got out of the driver's side, yelling at the people in the heavy-duty SUV.

The other driver got out and I heard the jeep guy yelp, reaching inside to grab something. Before he could reach it, Mr. SUV shoved him against the side and I heard a sickening crunch.

I froze, wondering what I should do. Next thing I knew, a second guy grabbed me and shoved me into the back of the stinky interior. He wore a mask, so I had no idea what he looked like, yet he still pulled a black bag over my head.

"Not a sound if you know what's good for ya." He had a thick southern accent. "Got her. Let's go."

"Right," the other man replied slamming the door shut.

I still had my keys, but evidently I'd dropped my mail. In the back of my mind I'd hoped maybe one of my neighbors had seen what happened and called the police. Maybe even gotten the license plates if I'd been lucky.

As the vehicle roared away, I hoped my cats would be all right.

~ * ~

Seeing the dropped mail on the sidewalk alarmed Bertram the moment he'd arrived. He picked it up seeing Cira's address. He caught the faint whiff of pine, and frowned, knowing of only one vampire who favored the scent. Chad Wodley. He worked for Lionel Martelli.

With a muttered curse he hurried to her door and pounded on the dark wood. He heard the cats scamper away, their tiny hearts thudding in fear. When she didn't answer, Bertram pulled out his lock picking kit. He'd learned the trick from a talented thief.

Letting himself in, he saw her laptop sitting on her black glass topped desk and heard the radio playing. Turning the music off, he quickly searched the house and found no trace of her. Her mail he left on the small table in her dining room. He examined the cards, noting the shoe scuff marks and smudged dirt.

Angry, he threw them back down and pulled out his cell phone. Glancing out the patio door, he saw the damaged jeep out front and wondered what had happened to the driver.

Two rings sounded in his ear, before a slightly accented gravelly voice answered. "What is it, Bertram?"

"Sorry to disturb you, Isaac, we have a problem."

"I'm listening."

Quickly he gave a brief description of what he'd found and his subsequent encounters with Martelli, including the man trying to drain Cira a few days earlier. "She has a rare blood type."

"Not good. You know what he'll do with her."

"You have the resources to track a potential sale." His stomach knotted at the thought of her ending up sold to some avid collector or worse case, a vampire who enjoyed the kill.

"What does she look like?" Isaac had gone into brisk business mode.

"I snapped a picture of her." He'd taken it while she'd been signing books on Friday night. He sent it to his old friend.

"Got it. I'll get this distributed immediately. There are those who owe me."

Bertram knew better than to ask.

"She's lovely," Isaac commented. Not often he noticed. "She's important to you?"

"More than I care to admit."

"Then I will endeavor to recover her for you." A brief silence. "Perhaps you have found your life mate as I have in my Rachel."

Had he? Bertram couldn't be sure. "She is...sweet." He wouldn't need to explain.

"Ah, tasted her, did you?" His creator chuckled. "Well, let us see what can be done."

"My business is completed. I'll have my pilot prep my jet and return in a few hours." He glanced up. Two sets of yellow eyes stared down from the loft. Probably annoyed he'd invaded their territory. Maybe he had. "First, I need to find a cat sitter. Cira will be heartbroken if anything happens to them."

"A moment." He heard keys clicking. "I have a number for you." He read it off. "Give my granddaughter a call and tell her I referred you."

Leave it to Isaac to have a contact related to him for any unexpected need. "Thank you."

"You can thank me when we find her. Huh." Isaac paused and Bertram waited. "Have a report of a hunter ending up in the ER. You may want to check it out. I'm texting you the hospital address."

"There is a damaged jeep sitting out front and I smelled pine."

"We both know who wears that scent."

"We do." He wanted to question the hunter to see if he seen or heard anything which could prove helpful. "I'll see you in a few hours."

"We'll be searching for her, have no fear of that." Isaac hung up.

Bertram made the call to the cat sitter, located a spare house key tucked into a tin and waited until the woman arrived. While he did so, he checked to see where the hospital was located.

A light knock interrupted him. A Goth chick waved at him, her black hair short and sprouting piercings in her nose, lip and several in her ears. She had on clothes matching her hair.

"You called for a sitter."

"I did. Thank you for coming." He caught the familiar scent of an older vampire human mix.

"No problem. Where are they?"

He pointed at the loft. Neither cat moved.

"They're cute. Name's June."

"I believe she keeps their stuff in the downstairs bathroom," he hurriedly told the young woman.

"Know their names?" She pointed up at the cats.

"Sorry, no." He'd never asked Cira and he felt awful for not doing so. He knew how important they were to her.

"I'll just call them kitty."

He handed her the key. "I have no idea how long this will take."

"Got it covered." She grinned. "Grandfather told me what happened. You go get that jerk who grabbed your girl. Reassure her I'm taking good care of her kitty babies." June winked. "No bill for this job, it's covered." She put her hand up when he started to protest. "No argument. Go get your girl."

~ * ~

The guy wearing the pine cologne just stank and the smell became stifling. I thought I would vomit. Be pretty disgusting inside the bag on my head.

Eventually the SUV stopped, and I got dragged out. At some point they'd put plastic ties on my wrists. A bit too tightly. They hurt.

"I told you to be gentle." I recognized the voice and wanted to scream.

The bag was pulled off and the ties cut loose.

I blinked as my eyes got used to the light and rubbed my sore wrists. We stood inside a huge hanger. A couple of small planes were parked along a wall and I saw a few people working at desks. Maybe if I yelled, they'd call for help.

"You don't want to do that," Martelli threatened. "I'd hate to have kill them all. Such a waste of blood."

His words scared me. I kept my mouth shut.

"Let's see." He grabbed my hands turning my arms over as he inspected them. "We need to get lotion on them. My buyers like their merchandise undamaged."

The two men leered at me. Again, I wanted to throw up.

"Get her in the plane. Be gentle!" he ordered.

Mr. Pine Scent grabbed my upper arm and forced me across the hanger to the small plane sitting outside. He pushed me up the ramp and pointed at the seat. He took a place near the back. The other man who had hurt the jeep guy sat nearby. Martelli followed, ordering the door to be shut.

"I trust you're comfortable, my dear." His smile reminded me of a serpent eating a rat.

"Not really," I retorted.

"I apologize for your rough handling. My orders specifically said you were not to be harmed in any way."

"Maybe I'll bring a lower price." I couldn't help baiting him.

He shook his head. Didn't he ever wear anything other than a fancy tailored suit and red tie? "They're more interested in your blood than your appearance, although we'll make you as attractive as possible."

"Thanks a lot," I snapped back.

"Spirted," he commented, sitting back in the peach velvet seat, his finger resting below his lower lip. "I have buyers who will want to tame you."

"What am I, a horse?"

"Not hardly. You'll fetch a high price."

"Wait a minute…" All his sentences began to make sense. "You're selling me?" I couldn't believe it. Sure, I knew this type of thing went on, but I never thought I'd see it in person, let alone be a piece of merchandise.

"I have a very lucrative business in finding those with rare blood types and selling them to selective buyers." He poured himself a glass of white wine. Sipping it he regarded me with dark eyes. "I've tasted you already."

My hand rubbed the spot where he'd bit me, fear beginning to fill me, causing my heart to speed up and my stomach to roll. Hand on my mouth and I looked frantically around.

"There." He pointed to the back of the plane as if my being ill was both expected and unimportant.

I ran back there, past his two goons and lost all the contents of my stomach. Shaking, I sat on the toilet and felt the plane lift into the air. With no idea where I'd be taken, I broke down and cried.

~ * ~

His jet had been in the air for two hours and his pilot had promised they'd be landing at Logan Airport in about another two, plus however long it took them before they'd get clearance to set down. Bertram spent the time researching what had been garnered about Martelli's trafficking routes and auction houses.

The talk he'd had with the hunter had proven unfruitful. His assailant had worn a ski mask and attacked so quickly the man, Jake, hadn't even had time to use his crossbow. Not that the arrow would have done him any good. Again, nonsense taken from films and TV. The hunter should have known better.

After their talk, Bertram had charmed the patient's full name from one of the nurses and would have his attorney anonymously pay the hospital bills. It was the least he could do, although the question arose of what had he been doing there in the first place and how had they known to watch Cira's home? A question he would seek the answer to another time.

His attention returned to the laptop screen. Martelli had holdings beginning in Maine, down the eastern seaboard, to the southeast and along the Gulf of Mexico. The only reason it hadn't gone further was because another powerful mobster held the west coast, and the Mexican vampires fiercely protected their territory.

Cira could be held in any number of places, yet his gut, based on their history, told him taking her had been personal. The one place Martelli would know Bertram would go was Boston, so he'd concentrate his search there and hope, maybe even pray despite his falling out with God, his guess proved correct.

~ * ~

"Have a nice nap, my lovely."

Shaking my head, I slowly pushed up from the couch I'd evidently fallen asleep on. A white fleece blanket had been thrown over me. I heard the goons laughing at whatever they were watching on the small TV embedded in the wall.

"We'll be landing shortly," Martelli informed me. His wine glass stood empty. "I've ordered you a meal that will be waiting for you when we arrive." Again, he grinned. "My driver will be picking us up."

"Where are we going?" My throat hurt and I needed a drink of water.

"Back to the one place I know Bertram will search for you."

He had to be taking me to Boston. "He won't come for me." I hoped the opposite but wanted to plant a seed of doubt in the vampire mobster's mind.

"Oh, he'll come for you." Martelli poured himself another glass of wine. "We go way back, Bertram and I."

I felt the plane shift. They must be circling. "Really? I had no idea."

"Quite a ways back." He finished his wine off in one gulp. "You see, I have a score to settle with him and taking you is just the beginning."

"Don't suppose you feel like sharing."

"Everything at its proper time." He pointed to the seat belt. "Best secure that."

With nothing else to do, I buckled the belt and prepared to land in the city I had always wanted to revisit. Not to live, though part of me was very tempted. Of course, this hadn't been part of my plan and I prayed I didn't disappear into the dark underbelly. Rats and all.

The wheels touched down and Martelli personally ushered me out over the blacktop and into a brown car with the windows tinted so darkly I couldn't see out. His goons didn't accompany us. Maybe he felt it safe enough and figured I wouldn't try to escape. Proved he doesn't know much about me.

Traffic can be either awful or not so bad, depending on the time of day. Most folks used the subway because it's the easiest way to get around. Parking could be extremely difficult if not unfindable. I remembered those little facts from living there previously.

I glanced at Martelli. He'd pulled out his cellphone and seemed preoccupied by the message on the screen. My fingers inched toward the handle. If I could see out, I might be able to choose my moment. All depended on whether or not the locks had been set. Should they be, making an escape would be impossible.

"Wouldn't try that if I were you." My hand stopped. "They're locked."

"Can't blame me for trying."

"And spoil my fun?" Martelli chuckled. I hated the way it sounded. "I have such plans for you, my dear."

"I don't think so." I tried to keep my voice steady despite my pounding heart.

His fingers locked around my neck. "You listen to me, human. I've been planning my revenge for a long, long time. Don't try to deny it to me." His fingers loosened. "I won't hesitate to take you myself if you prove to be too much trouble." With a leering grin his eyes looked me up and down. "And I'm not just talking about your blood."

I tried to suppress the shudder running through my body. If he meant what I thought, then I needed to do everything I could to prevent it. My eyes dropped and I clinched my hands in my lap.

"That's a good girl." He patted my leg, inching his fingers up my thigh and dangerously close to the place only my ex-husband had touched. "Although, you are a rare beauty. Never any harm in trying the sample."

He leaned toward me. I had to think of a reason to throw him off...or...

The car swerved, disrupting Martelli's balance. He grabbed at the seat to balance himself. "What the hell was that?"

"Sorry, sir, debris in the road," the driver apologized.

The Italian glared at me before returning his attention to his phone.

I sighed in relief and fought tears, although they escaped down my cheeks. His lust and desire hadn't ebbed, covering me in a shameful blanket. I dreaded what he would do to me when we arrived, wherever we were going.

~ * ~

Isaac had sent a car for him and Bertram had no idea how he'd thank his old friend. The driver wearing a black uniform, Abe if he remembered correctly, opened the back door. He slid inside, surprised to find his creator sitting on the brown leather seat.

"Martelli landed an hour ago," Isaac informed him. He'd cut his silver hair again, his pale blue eyes meeting Bertram's, giving him a curious look. "No tie?"

"Cira doesn't like them." He wondered why and would make a point of asking her once he safely had her back.

His mentor though, had a keen insight. "Has that much influence does she?"

"I don't mind pleasing her."

"Bedded her yet?"

"No." Isaac's straight forward questions didn't normally bother Bertram. Asking whether or not he'd bedded Cira did for some reason he couldn't quite understand.

"Hmmm." Isaac motioned the driver to go. "We have a tail on Martelli. He went to his Somerville triple decker."

"Not his home in the Back Bay?"

"Apparently not."

"How soon can we go in?"

"You know how it works."

A summons or a challenge. Martelli would be counting on one of them or both being issued. The prize, if the latter, Cira, and other terms they'd agree upon beforehand.

Bertram considered the possibility. "Might be our only chance at rescuing her." And perhaps the only chance he'd have to take down the mobster's network.

"Risky." Isaac regarded him, his eyes narrowed slightly. "Are you sure you want to do that?"

Isaac knew about the fallout the two men had back in the early eighteen hundreds, but not the details. They'd never been shared. Bertram pushed the memory of their argument away. Now was not the time. "Very."

"I'll gather the Elders and issue a summons." Isaac sat back in the seat. "Even Martelli is unable to deny coming. If he did, he'd forfeit his life."

He knew the terms of a summons, grateful his friend had repeated them. "She has to be protected no matter the outcome." Bertram couldn't keep the worry out of his voice.

Looking sympathetic, Isaac looked at Bertram. "Only one way

to do that. You'll need her consent."

"I'll need time with her in order to secure it. Martelli is not about to grant me that." He knew why, understanding the past could not be undone.

"Might be able to arrange it," Isaac mused. "Depending on when the challenge is set."

"I can also take her by force." He cringed at the thought not wanting to hurt Cira. "I would rather not."

"Best you don't." They pulled up in front of Isaac's home, a two-story traditional Colonial. He and his wife had lived there since before the Revolutionary war. Bertram had been their guest many times. "I see my wife is waiting for me," Isaac said with a fond smile on his face.

"I should let you go to her."

"Will you be staying as our guest or going home?"

He'd bet Martelli would be watching his home. Isaac's too. "If you don't mind, I'd like to stay."

"Good idea. Once Rachel is informed of your plan, she may be able to give you an approach, which will work with the woman who has obviously won your heart."

"I've listened to your wife's wisdom many times." The important words Isaac had just uttered began to sink in. Had Cira indeed won his affections?

"In this matter," Isaac continued. "It will be the most important advice you will ever receive."

~ * ~

Martelli locked me in the back bedroom, after I'd been forced into the shower and a change of clothes. Glancing around I saw the mattress on the hardwood floor, with what looked like clean sheets and a large quilt. At least, I hoped the sheets were clean.

A small table with a tray of covered food and a pot of tea waited for me and I sat down on the hard chair. I ate the salad, piece of chicken and the brownie. I sipped the tea, placing the cup on the table to check out the three windows. They all had bars on them. *Drat!*

I tried the door, though I remembered seeing it had a bar across it. In one corner sat a small mobile toilet, plus paper and wipes. Seems my captor had thought of everything.

Sitting back down, I tried not to sink into despair. In the movies and books, this is when the hero charges in and rescues the damsel in distress. I doubted it would happen in real life. After all, Bertram had no idea where I was.

Other than being in Somerville, even I wasn't exactly sure where. I lived in the town for a couple of years. Didn't know every square inch of the suburb although something about this house seemed familiar. Maybe because it was a triple decker or maybe, just maybe, it might be the same house I'd lived in. Coincidences can happen.

The door opened and Martelli entered, closing it behind him. "We were rudely interrupted earlier."

Thinking fast and betting on his motives, I rose to my feet, looking him straight in the eye. "You said you wanted revenge on him right?"

He stared at me, wanting me. I could physically feel his lust, yet he was curious what I would suggest. "Whatever you're planning, wouldn't it be better to take me while he watched and is helpless to stop you?" *What in the world was I saying!*

He rubbed his gnarled hands together. "I like the way you think." Martelli took a step towards me. I stood my ground. The Italian continued, "Don't think in the end I won't have you. Bertram Hoel is no shining prince," he snarled.

"I don't believe in princes."

"Good thing." With a smirk, he added. "I like the idea of watching him squirm while I take the one thing *he* wants away from him before I relieve him of his head."

So at least one part of vampire lore is true. Behead a vampire and he dies.

"I'm sure the process is moving forward and the summons I'm expecting will arrive by dawn. Might as well get some sleep, my dear. I have little intention of allowing you much after Bertram Hoel is dead."

Chapter 7
Blood Marriage

Isaac dispensed the messenger with the summons for Martelli. Odd to think the hunters would, Bertram reflected, run errands for the vampires, particularly the Elders.

"Can you trust him?" Bertram asked, from his chair next to the brick fireplace.

"No more than you can any human." His old friend sipped the tea his wife had served. The cup he held would be considered an antique and fetch a high price, should the couple decide to part with what had been presented to them as a wedding gift. Bertram remembered since he'd attended the ceremony.

Restless, his eyes glanced around the room. Bertram had been there many times. A red velvet Victorian couch graced the living room sitting on the hardwood floor along with matching chairs beside the fireplace. Vases full of flowers and candles sat on hand carved oak tables. Lace curtains adorned the window staring out on the quiet street.

"Worried about the summons?" Isaac asked, sitting back on the couch.

"Concerned I'm doing exactly what he wants." He worried what Martelli could be doing to Cira. Had he raped her yet? Or tasted her blood? Or sold her? Each fate made him ball his fists tighter as his fury grew.

"You must care for her a great deal." Isaac placed the empty cup and saucer gently on the low coffee table. "I can see by your stance, and your hands are a dead giveaway."

"I know what he could be doing to her."

The older man smiled. "He won't harm her until he has what he wants." His eyes drifted to the archway as he wife Rachel joined them. "My dear."

She smiled at her husband. Several years younger, her auburn hair had just begun to gray when her husband had turned her.

Rachel wore her skirts long, no doubt because old habits were hard to break, Bertram mused. She sat on the couch and regarded

~ 67 ~

the men. "Is the subject so weighty I am not welcome?" Her brown eyes held a hint of mischief.

"You are more than welcome, my love," Isaac returned, taking her hand. "We have a matter needing your wisdom."

"Ah, this concerns a woman." She nodded, her gaze sympathetic. "Please, enlighten me."

Isaac looked at Bertram expectantly. The younger vampire desperately wanted to be banging on doors to find Cira, not waiting to hear back about the terms of her release, as if Martelli would let her go.

"I'll be issuing a challenge," Bertram began.

Rachel regarded him calmly. "Have you considered your terms?"

"I have." If Martelli won, he'd take over all of Bertram's business holdings, homes and bank accounts. "I have one condition he will fight me on."

"The woman." She crossed her feet at the ankle. "What is your wish there?"

"She isn't a piece of property and I have no right to make her one." He got up and began to pace. "There is but one option."

"Such has not been done for four hundred years."

Bertram didn't know if he should be relieved or not his friend's wife knew exactly what he meant. "I'm well aware."

"Daring move." She looked at her husband. "Martelli will not be expecting it."

"He will need time with her to gain her consent," Isaac told her with a shared look of understanding.

"So, she's still human." Rachel gazed at Bertram like a mother would.

The scientist nodded.

"It will need to be explained to her simply and hope she understands the implications and possible consequences," Rachel said thoughtfully.

Did he? The more Bertram thought about it, the more uncertain he became. "I'm not even sure I do."

Isaac spoke, "That you're even considering it, means you do."

"Will the Elders back my decision?" They would be the only thing preventing him from carrying out his daring plan.

"My cousin, Jacob will be arriving shortly with his wife Naomi.

I will speak to them both."

Getting to her feet, Rachel asked, "Do we know where he's keeping her?"

"I have eyes on him," her husband replied.

"Good. T'will make things easier." Her eyes caught Bertram's. "I think Martelli will not object if I speak to her. Do you agree?"

Knowing he had no choice, and Martelli would not be able to say no to an Elder's request, Bertram nodded.

~ * ~

From experience, Lance knew it could be risky running an errand for a vamp. Still, the Boston hunters who were willing would do so for the Elders. Most of them came from families who had fought, bled and died for the freedom of the country. Yes, it happened well over two hundred years ago. Still, their important sacrifice meant everything given Boston's historical significance and role in the Revolutionary war.

Pulling his car into the tight driveway, Lance got out and pounded on the white door. The house had recently been redone and painted a dark blue gray. The door opened and he entered, aware the vamp might kill him.

"You have it," the olive-skinned man asked.

"Here." He handed the document to him.

Unrolling the parchment, he read the words and a smile spread across his craggy face. "Excellent." His chocolate eyes looked at Lance. "Here are my terms." He pulled an envelope out of his pocket. "Return this to your master."

Taking it, he saw Isaac Rosen's name scrawled on it. He glared at the vamp. "The Elder is not my master."

"You do his bidding."

"Let us just say, we have an understanding." No need to make himself a target.

The other dismissed him with a wave of his hand. "No matter."

"The woman," he began.

"She is of no concern to you." He began to close the door.

"I have been instructed to check on her welfare. If you refuse, then you automatically forfeit."

The vamp's eyes burned red, and Lance couldn't be sure if Martelli would agree or not. "Very well," he huffed. Stomping across the hallway to the back of the house, he opened a barred door. "One minute.'"

Lance slipped inside. A woman turned to face him. She looked tired and frightened, but at least, from the empty tray sitting on a small table, they'd been feeding her. The image of the fatted calf before the feast flitted through his head and he hoped it wouldn't be her fate.

"You okay?"

She shrugged. "As I can be."

"Just know your release is being negotiated."

"At what price?"

"Not my place to know."

"Time!" A rough hand pulled him out. "Satisfied?"

"Thank you." Better to be polite than eaten as dinner. "Tell the Elders I will be there at the appointed hour."

"You're to bring the woman."

The vamp's eyes flashed a deep red again.

"It's in the summons," Lance pointed at the parchment.

"Get out!"

Not daring to speak, he hastily left, closing the door behind him. Getting back in his car, he made the call to Isaac Rosen. "Delivered. I have his terms."

"I appreciate your help."

"Tell Dr. Hoel she's alive and from what I can tell unharmed."

"I'll let him know."

"I should be back within the hour." He started the car. "Just do me a favor, make sure Martelli loses his head."

~ * ~

The elders had gathered in Isaac's living room. Bertram stood slightly behind his creator, near the archway. Rachel sat beside her husband on the couch. Both had changed into more formal clothes, Isaac a black suit and his wife a purple gown.

An extra chair had been brought in and Isaac's cousin Jacob Rosen sat there, his wife seated in the one next to him. Jacob too, wore a suit, his gray hair slicked back and smelling slightly of grease. Naomi, a handsome woman with peppered hair, moved restlessly in her green dress.

In the other chair near the fireplace sat Deborah Metcalf. She made no pretense of belonging to the twenty-first century. Her colonial brown dress and her piled black hair seemed to fit her well.

Around the rest of the room a few others stood, waiting to hear why the meeting had been called.

Isaac quickly filled in with the events as Bertram had shared them. Watching the room, he tried to determine their reactions, guessing who may or not, support his daring plan.

"Interesting," Deborah said her hands folded neatly in her lap. "A very daring plan young Bertram." She leaned stiffly forward. "Have you considered the consequences?"

"As much as I can," he honestly answered.

The front door opened, and he heard hurried footsteps through the entry way. The human, Lance as Bertram remembered, who had been sent to deliver the summons, handed an envelope to Isaac. "We'll be there if you need us," he said, before leaving the room and exiting the house.

Opening the envelope Isaac read the terms, his eyes narrowing. He said nothing as he handed it to Bertram who quickly read it and growled.

"Martelli will be here at the appointed hour," he informed the room.

"He wants the woman," Deborah astutely surmised.

Isaac nodded. "This may be more difficult than we thought."

~ * ~

The door opened and I steeled myself for what might come next. Martelli stood there in his finest and frowned at me. "You can't go dressed like that." He pointed at the short robe I wore.

"Go where?" I dared to ask.

"To the summons of course." Like I should know what that is. He turned to the servant, or so I assumed, behind him who carried a beautiful sapphire gown. "Please shower and change. You'll find everything you need in the bathroom."

I took the dress from the meek looking man, who stared at the hardwood floor, and ducked into the bathroom, locking the door. The sound of the click made me happy, and I quickly showered and changed.

At least my captor proved correct. He'd provided lotion, makeup, and hair stuff. I used a simple braid fastening it with a shining barrette, its shade matching the dress. I slipped on the flats happy to see them. I hated heels.

Stepping out of the room, I found Martelli waiting for me in the small cozy living room. It had a white fireplace with furniture the same shade. The couch had red pillows tossed on it and a rug the same hue on the hardwood floor.

"You look lovely," Martelli complimented.

His look made me hope I wasn't the main course. I tried not to react to his compliment.

He moved behind me and I felt coldness on my neck. Moving to stand in front of me he handed me the box. "The matching earrings."

"You don't mind if I use the bathroom mirror."

"Of course not."

I returned to the room and put them on. Sparkling jewels hung from my ears and throat. Clear and probably diamonds. I didn't think he'd go for any type of cheap copy.

"If you're ready, my dear."

I jumped, not having heard him. "This will keep you warm." He placed a heavy white cloak around my shoulders. "Can't have you getting cold."

Once again he put me in the back of his car, unable to see the streets or our destination. I sat back against seat and tried to relax, my apprehension growing by the moment. "Where are we going?" I asked surprised my voice didn't squeak.

"To see the Elders." He smiled as if he had planned the entire event and it was being presented for his amusement.

I wondered what my role in it would be. "And where are these Elders?"

"Brookline," he answered, reaching out and snagging my hand. "You will be silent."

"Why?"

"You will be silent," he repeated, squeezing my fingers until it hurt.

I nodded, biting my lower lip so I wouldn't cry out or speak.

He patted my hand, like I was a pet dog and had just done a trick for him. "Good girl."

Martelli didn't talk to me again during the whole trip. When we arrived, he ushered me out of the car and up the stairs to the porch done very much in the style of Colonial days. I could tell, even in the dark, the house had been painted white.

"Remember," he warned me. "Not a word."

The door swung open as if his arrival had been expected. Stepping inside, he acted as if he were king of the castle. A quiet girl dressed in a maid's outfit took my cloak and scurried away.

I followed my captor into the living room filled with people who, although they had dressed in modern clothes, except for one woman, none of them really seemed to fit in this century. Not sure how I could tell. Maybe by the way they felt.

"Thank you for coming, Martelli," a voice greeted.

My eyes darted to the couch. An older man and woman sat there and I would have bet they owned the house. Behind them stood Bertram and I smiled at him. He cast a look at Martelli as if to caution me. I took the hint.

"You've read my terms." The Italian sounded almost gleeful.

"No challenge has formally been issued," the man continued. "Why did you think it necessary to send them?"

Martelli turned to Bertram, a half grin on his face. "Because one will be issued." Taking a step forward, he stared right at him ignoring everyone else in the room. "I challenge you, Bertram Hoel, not just for your holdings, but for the woman Cira Landon as well."

"I have one condition," Bertram responded, looking calm and in command. "You allow Rachel Rosen to speak with Ms. Landon in private."

"For what purpose?" my captor demanded.

A woman spoke up who I assumed was Rachel. "To ensure no harm has come to her."

"You mean to make certain I haven't *taken* her." His tone left no question what he meant.

Rachel rose and straightened proudly. She looked regal in her purple dress. "If you must speak in such crass words, then yes."

"You will hear my terms," Bertram interjected.

"They are hardly important," Martelli retorted, "Since you will not live to see the dawn."

"Should I win," Bertram continued as if Martelli hadn't spoken. "I will take your fortune, homes and property and I warn you." His eyes burned bright red. "I will dismantle your trafficking rings and criminal empire."

"As I said, it is of no concern." He turned to me. "You may speak with Rachel."

With a nod I followed her out of the room into the kitchen. It proved to be quite homey, if a bit old fashioned. The appliances were all white and seemed to date back to the early 1920s or 1930s. A couple of dog dishes sat next to the sink.

She motioned me to follow her out the back door onto a porch. "Please be seated."

I settled into the tan wicker chair and waited for her to ask me questions I'd bet would be embarrassing. Her cool hand rested on mine. "You need not be afraid, my dear."

Why did everyone call me 'my dear'? For some reason it annoyed me. "My name is Cira."

"So Bertram told us."

"Have you known him a long time?" I wanted to know.

"For much of his life." Rachel's voice held warmth. "I must share a thing of importance with you."

"Will it keep me out of Martelli's bed?" I couldn't help the shudder going through my body.

"The purpose is that it will give you rights," she informed me.

Two dogs barked and ran up on the porch. Their tails wagged. I had no idea what breed they were, probably both mutts, one black and the other brown with a white patch on its forehead. Rachel took a moment to scratch behind their ears. She reached into a colorful tin handing each a treat. They dashed down the stairs and disappeared behind the bushes in the good-sized yard.

"I'm surprised you have pets."

"Isaac has always loved dogs. It pleases him so it pleases me."

"You sound fond of him."

She laughed. "I should hope so. We have been married for well over two hundred years"

"You've been married for..." I couldn't believe what I had just heard.

"Jacob and Naomi have been together almost as long."

I had no idea who they were in the room filled with the vampire Elders. "Am I the only human here?"

"For the moment." Rachel's eyes sought out mine. "A formal challenge has been issued." She paused, a sad look on her face. "Both men knew it would happen."

"Challenge?"

She sighed. "From time-to-time disagreements happen. This is how they are settled." She shook her head. "We've been expecting this for years unfortunately."

"Do you know why?"

"Not the details. It would be better if Bertram told you." She patted my hand. "Now, I must share with you what must happen, since your consent will be needed."

~ * ~

When the two women returned, Bertram saw the drawn expression on Cira's face. Her gray eyes darted in his direction and then away. He saw her hands tremble and smelled her fear. Damn! He hadn't wanted her frightened.

"So," Isaac sat back, his blue eyes facing the room. "What is the decision Martelli? Dr. Hoel?"

"Dr. Hoel," Martelli mocked. "I challenge you again per the terms I sent, including her!" He pointed at Cira.

Bertram answered Martelli's challenge. "My terms have been named. I set the time at midnight."

"I accept. An hour will hardly make a difference," the other scoffed.

Bertram smiled. "Will it not?" He stepped from his place at Isaac's side, seeing his old friend nod in agreement and stood in the center of the room. "I claim the woman Cira Landon as my blood bride."

"You can't!" the mobster objected, fury mottling his face.

"He can," Rachel informed him. "For he has not yet accepted your challenge." Martelli started to object. "Bertram has accepted your terms, set his and the time, as is his right." Her attention focused on Cira giving the woman a slight nod.

Bertram waited for her answer, almost afraid to hear it. "What say you, Cira?" he asked.

Cira cast a frightened look at Martelli. No doubt he'd warned her about speaking and his actions angered Bertram.

"He has no right to keep you silent." Rachel sent a warning look at Martelli. "You may speak."

"No, she can't!" he bellowed.

"You would dare contradict an Elder?" Not often did Rachel

use the dangerous tone Bertram heard. To do so would cost the mobster all he had and his life. Bertram waited to see how far Martelli would push.

"Of course not," he consented giving Rachel a half bow, his expression resentful. Jacob moved from his chair to stand beside the mobster, probably to prevent him from interfering. Bertram appreciated the gesture.

Isaac spoke, "You have been asked a question, Miss Landon. What say you?"

Her tongue darted out to wet her lower lip. She gazed around the room, her cheeks flushing red. "I," She swallowed before trying again. "I agree to be his blood bride."

With her consent, Isaac rose and took her hand, leading her over to Bertram. "Give me your hand." He complied. Quietly his creator said, "This must be done publicly before the Elders. You may not take her until after the challenge has been accepted and fought. Whatever the outcome."

Cira looked at the floor, her cheeks bright red.

Putting their hands together, he told Bertram. "You know what must be done." His old friend returned to his wife's side.

"Unbutton my shirt," he told Cira.

"Do what?" Her gray eyes echoed her surprise.

"Unbutton my shirt," he repeated, trying to keep his patience with her. Bertram knew what had to be done. It was the only protection he could offer Cira. He undid the flashy diamond necklace and removed the matching earrings, dropping them to the floor. They landed with a quiet thud. Martelli's snarl gave him pleasure.

"I noticed you'd lost your tie," she teased, her shaking fingers undoing the buttons. "Rachel wasn't too specific on how far this might go," she whispered.

"I will do nothing that will compromise you," he promised. "I want to make it as pleasant as possible."

"A whole room full of vampires watching us and I'm supposed to enjoy what you're doing?" Her voice expressed her disbelief.

"Close your eyes and pretend we're alone."

"Except we're not."

"Cira," he breathed, bringing his mouth down on hers. He heard her gasp and her body stiffen in response. Bertram drew her into his arms, continuing his kiss until her lips parted slightly. His tongue darted in, tasting her, feeling her beginning to relax.

His hands moved along her back, although he ached to touch her more intimately, the dress she wore making it difficult to control his desire. He knew they had an audience and he'd made her a promise. She trembled in his arms and he gently ended the kiss, moving his lips along her jaw and slowly down her throat, a soft fragrance of vanilla filling his nose.

Cira moaned, her body relaxing against him. He felt her heart beating against his bare chest and briefly he regretted what he had to do. Knowing there was no other choice, he sank his fangs into her throat, and heard her whimper in pain. Her sweet blood, which he had tasted before, rushed into his mouth, reminding him of apple pie.

He drank slowly, savoring the rich flavor, draining her. Her heart slowed, paused, beat again.

He lowered himself into a seated position, pulling her onto his lap. Isaac appeared with a blade and put it in Bertram's hand. Her heart stuttered, straining to keep her alive.

With one thrust, Bertram buried the blade in his chest, removing it so his blood would flow freely and directly from his heart.

"NO!" Martelli yelled, lunging to stop the marriage.

Jacob and Isaac both restrained him. "Hurry!" Isaac urged, as the mobster struggled against the two Elders, howling in protest.

Bertram raised Cira's head enough to put her mouth against the wound. "Drink," he urged. "Two swallows at least."

Her hand weakly touched his chest, pressing her mouth against him. He felt her draw his blood and swallow. Once. Twice. Three times, before she collapsed in his arms.

He listened as her heart took a final beat before it stopped and her body went limp.

Raising his pain filled eyes he met Martelli's furious ones. "I accept your challenge."

~ * ~

Not sure how I can describe the mixed impressions I sensed upon waking. The firm mattress under my back. Covers over my still fully clothed body except my shoes. I had no idea where they went. A sharp awareness of a body near mine smelling of sea water and another musky odor I couldn't identify, making me want to, I blushed thinking about it.

The strongest deep hunger cutting like shards of glass into my stomach and pinching my legs and arms. With a groan I tried to sit up only managing to curl into a tight ball, the covers pulled into knot.

"Easy," I recognized the voice, as his warmish fingers brushed my hair out of my face, his weight settling on the bed next to me. "Rachel!"

Steps as loud as sonic booms approached, and I wanted to cover my ears. I sobbed my agony.

"Here, child," the woman urged. "Help her sit up, Bertram."

Strong arms around me, pulling my tightened limbs straight, supporting my aching body against his still bare chest. "Drink this," he ordered as he forced a cup against my lips. Warm coppery liquid dribbled in my mouth, sliding down my throat, settling into my complaining stomach and calming the unbearable pain. I drank the entire amount, craving more as he pulled it away.

"Slowly at first," he told me, his hand rubbing my back. "Let the blood do its work."

The pain slowly eased and I gasped in relief.

Bertram asked, "Feeling better?"

I nodded, not able to speak yet.

The two exchanged a look. Rachel moved a chair next to the bed. "You made the right decision."

Flashes through my mind as my fingers crawled to touch my neck. I vaguely remembered being bitten, an odd mix of pleasure and pain.

"You're like me now," Bertram told me.

"What do you mean?" I croaked. My jumbled thoughts attempting to process what had happened in the living room.

"I believe you've written your fair share of vampire stories." Rachel smiled at me as if I were her favorite daughter. "Oh, we're quite familiar with your work."

Great. Vamps who've read my stories.

"How much was right?" I heard myself ask.

"You have a keen insight." Her cool hand patted mine. "I will leave you to Bertram. These next few days will be difficult as you adjust." Rachel gave him a meaningful expression.

"My cats…" They bounced into my head. Animals, or so I had

noticed, were more aware of the supernatural than humans.

"They should be fine," Rachel assured me. "We've always had an understanding with them."

What an odd thing to say. My muddled mind couldn't comprehend what she meant.

"Cira's strong enough to attend," Rachel said. "We both know Martelli won't wait much longer."

My eyes focused on the clock on the nightstand. Eleven fifty. Almost midnight!

She pushed the chair back. "I'll let myself out, Bertram. Try to be in the yard at the appointed time." Rachel left us, the door closing with a soft click.

"Feel really…different."

Bertram sighed, moving off the bed. My body missed him and I shook my head. The scientist rubbed the back of his neck. His exposed hairy chest made me want to run my fingers all over it. I noticed an inch-long scar right about where his heart should be.

He must have noticed my gaze. "The scar won't disappear. It's a reminder of the promise I made to you."

"I'm still a bit confused."

He paced, his action making him seem more human. "Vampires exchange blood for few reasons, to turn another or make love." His eyes glowed a golden brown briefly. Bertram wanted me and I him. "Or take a mate."

Rachel had explained all this, yet why was I suddenly angry? I balled my fists wanting to pound on his chest or at the very least throw a vase or anything breakable. Settling for a pillow I tossed it across the room. It hit him and fell to the floor.

"I suppose I should be grateful it was something soft." A slight smile touched his full lips.

I dropped my face into my hands. Me. A vampire bride. Not only could I not believe it, but the outcome also broke my heart, despite Rachel's attempt to prepare me. I began to weep.

Before I even became aware of him, Bertram sat at my side, holding me in his arms. "I'm so sorry," he whispered.

"Martelli?" I managed to sob out.

"That is the fight yet to come."

Leaning my head against my husband, a term that would take some time for me to get used to after being single for a number of years, I felt oddly safe, despite the unusual circumstance. "So now what?"

"We attend the challenge." I heard a bit of doubt in his voice. "Afterward, we'll get to know each other and when you're ready," he spoke so quietly I almost didn't hear him. "I hope you'll join me in my bed."

"Get out." I pushed him away.

"You're expected to attend," he said quietly as he opened the door. "Be in the back yard at midnight."

I listened to him leave, not wanting him to. My feelings so mixed I couldn't figure out how to make sense of them. Rising, I found a small bathroom attached, rinsed by face, and left the room.

Rachel waited for me at the bottom of the stairs, her eyes sympathetic. "The first few days are the worst," she told me.

"Nice," I muttered, not looking forward to it. "I suppose I have to worry about sunlight."

The older woman laughed. "Only in the movies."

~ * ~

His eyes flew to the back door as Cira and Rachel joined them. They came down the stairs and took chairs so they both would have a clear view of the challenge. Other Elders sat or stood, each so they could watch the movements of the two combatants. Isaac's dogs barked from behind the bushes. His creator had secured them in a pen earlier.

Lights had been strung to illuminate the area designated as the fight zone. Blades of all sizes hung from a constructed line reminding him this fight would end in only one way, his death or Martelli's.

Both men braced on bare feet, their upper torso naked. Both wore pants, a modern change to protect the women from seeing what they shouldn't. He'd heard that during ancient days they'd worn nothing at all.

Isaac stood between. "You are both certain of this?"

"Yes," Martelli growled.

"It's been agreed." Bertram had mixed emotions yet knew this must happen.

"So be it," Isaac continued. "You have both agreed to each other's terms, with one exception." The older man grinned.

Martelli threw angry eyes at Cira and then at Bertram. "You'll regret what you've done," he hissed.

"I doubt that," Bertram shot back. "In the unlikely event I lose, she can challenge and name a champion."

His opponent snorted. "No one here can defeat me."

At least Cira had protection. He knew Isaac and Rachel would look after her.

"If you two are quite through." Isaac glared at them both. "Begin." He stepped away, going to stand next to his wife.

Bertram dodged the charge he saw coming and pushed Martelli into the bushes. Startled, the other vampire yelped and floundered in the thorn covered branches. The dogs barked hysterically. His move gave him the element of surprise and he reached the weapons first, selecting a katana, before having to dodge a well-aimed thrust from a Roman short sword.

"Marvelous weapon," the Italian boasted. "Both sides extremely sharp." Blood dripped from the numerous briar scratches he'd received. "I'll have your woman yet," he vowed.

"Not without her consent." The penalty for taking a vampire woman against her will could be severe, ranging from being forced to be her slave to having his manhood removed.

"What do I care about that?" He hacked at Bertram who raised his to deflect the blow. Both of them had some training, but the era of needing to defend themselves with blades had passed. "This is going to be short fight," Martelli taunted. "Why not just give up and I'll kill you swiftly. See," he pointed the blade at Dr. Hoel's belly. "I've marked you already."

Glancing down, he saw the long shallow cut already beginning to heal since he'd drank Cira's blood. The only advantage he might have.

"I kept in practice!" the vampire gloated coming at him, a blur of thrusts and jabs.

Bertram retreated, wishing he'd done the same, being used to defending himself with words. His skill might tip the challenge in Martelli's favor. Good thing he'd taken Cira as a blood bride. It might prove to be her only protection.

~ * ~

I have no idea how long the fight continued. Both men panted, tiring, while the dogs continued to bark and yip. Martelli kept pushing, forcing Bertram to go on the defensive. My husband faltered and fell, his sword sliding across the ground and out of reach. I watched in horror as he tried to reach it, the mobster planting his dirty foot firmly on Bertram's chest and grinding as if squishing a bug.

"Now, we'll see about who claims your woman." Martelli raised his weapon for the final blow.

Next thing I knew I was running. I grabbed a short light sword off the rack and swung it to counter the strike. The weapons collided with a loud clang and I dropped the blade, my hands tingling from the impact.

"How dare you!" Martelli's fist impacted on my cheek, knocking me to the ground. I shook my head trying to clear it.

Out of the corner of my eye, I saw movement. Bertram scrambled to his feet, managing to reclaim his original sword. With a roar he attacked Martelli, hacking off his hand. Blood spurted and I scuttled back to escape the gore, probably getting grass stains on the blue dress I'd been forced to wear.

Howling in pain, the Italian tried to defend himself. I saw Bertram move forward on his leg as he swung his sword sideways. The sharp blade sliced through the other's neck and I saw a brief shocked expression, before Martelli's head tumbled off and bounced to the ground. The body dropped like an afterthought.

No one made a sound. Even the dogs fell silent.

Bertram tossed the sword as far away as he could before he hurried to my side. "Are you all right?"

I nodded, rubbing my jaw, wondering if vampires bruised.

"If you were not Bertram's blood bride," Isaac said as he joined us. "I'd have you killed, Cira."

"I take it that's not allowed." I hadn't even thought about the consequences of interfering.

"Under normal circumstances no."

My husband sagged to his knees, gasping in pain. I knelt beside him, aware of the multiple deep cuts, bleeding faster than they healed.

"What do we need to do?" I asked.

Isaac looked grim and I tried not to panic. Wouldn't do Bertram any good if I did.

"Luckily, we are prepared."

From his tone I decided it would be better not to ask. The

Elder aided Bertram to his feet. "Go with Rachel," he ordered me. "She'll make certain you're fed." He gave me a wry smile. "You'll need it."

Considering the pain I felt, I had no doubt. For now, I wouldn't argue with him.

~ * ~

He hated to kill when he took blood. Bertram avoided it at all costs if possible. Tonight, he'd had no choice. The man brought to him had been caught after murdering a couple and their child. Isaac forced the prisoner to his knees. "The price for taking innocent lives is death."

"Ya can't do this," the human objected.

"Since we caught you, we can." His eyes locked with Bertram's. "You know what you need to do."

Grabbing the murderer by the throat, he felt the terror of the man. Faintly, he felt regret, yet the Elders had already decided the murderer's fate. Raw need took over and he plunged his fangs deeply into the flesh, draining a few swallows at a time so he'd get the most nourishment.

When the other died, he dropped the body to the bedroom floor. Isaac motioned to a servant who would remove the carcass. "Best you take a shower and clean up. You have a bride to please this night." His old friend left him alone in the same bedroom Cira had awakened in earlier.

Showering, he washed the stench of battle and death off. He found fresh clothes awaiting him and grinned, knowing he always kept a few belongings there just in case. After he dressed, he went in search of Cira. He found her in the kitchen with Rachel.

Her gray eyes locked with his and he read relief in them. She rose from the table and came to him, reaching out to run her fingers through his beard. "Do I want to know?"

"No," he replied, catching her hand and kissing the palm.

"Then I won't ask."

Rachel spoke, "I have the guest room made up for you and I'm sure you know the way." She gave him a knowing look.

"I do." Taking his wife's hand, he led her up the carpeted stairs to a room at the back of house. Opening the door, he swung her off her feet and carried her inside, using his foot to close the door.

"What do you think you're doing?" Cira demanded.

He placed her on the bed. She moved away from him to the other side. "You may have Isaac's permission to 'take me' as he so eloquently put it." Cira hugged herself as if shielding her body. "But you don't have mine."

His body craved the feel of her and he had to control his strong desire to force himself on her. "I have never taken a woman against her will."

"Oh, really! And just have many women have you 'taken'?" He saw the regret in her eyes after she'd said the words.

"You already know the answer." His fatigue from battle began to descend. He rubbed his eyes. "I'm too tired to fight with you right now."

"Vampires actually get tired?" She didn't sound like she believed it.

"They do." He pulled off his clothes and laid them over a chair, not ashamed of his nakedness.

"What do you think you're doing?" Cira demanded, even as her eyes roved over his body before looking away.

"Going to bed." He crawled under the covers. "I suggest you do the same since I'm taking you home tomorrow."

"Hope you mean my real home." He felt her weight move and sounds of her undressing. Moments later she settled in, putting as much distance between them as she could.

"I promise you this," he assured her. "I will not make love to you unless you ask."

"That might be awhile."

"It'll be hard." Cira had no idea how much! "I will wait until you're ready."

He heard a sniffle and wondered if she was crying. His arms ached to hold her.

"I'm sorry," she said softly. "I'm just so overwhelmed. Like I had no real choice in all this."

"I'll give you the time you need." He would hate every moment of it.

"Thank you." She turned her back to him. "Night."

"Good night." He closed his eyes and drifted off into the twilight sleep, only he never dreamed.

Chapter 8
After the Challenge

Isaac hated breaking the Sabbath. For him it was Saturday rather than the traditional Sunday. He needed to meet with the leader of the hunters, Lance. He didn't know the man's last name and had never asked. It seemed better to keep their relationship all business. No need to get attached to humans with their short life spans.

Lance ducked into the carriage house and crossed his arms over his thick upper body. He had blond hair and piercing blue eyes. As normal, he wore jeans with a red and black checked, long sleeved shirt. "Heard Martelli lost his head."

"You heard correctly," Isaac answered. "Bertram was more merciful than I would have been."

"Seems everyone hated him."

"I'm certain his customers are aware and have taken their business elsewhere."

"Wouldn't count on it. There's always an ambitious second in command lurking about waiting for their chance."

"I think they'll find Dr. Hoel a force to be reckoned with."

"We can only hope." Lance leaned against the door. "Isn't Dr. Hoel more of an academic?"

"He's a guest professor at many colleges worldwide along with creating solutions for difficult problems."

"Has a wife now."

Isaac blinked taken back the hunter already knew. "We have tried to keep their union secret."

"You know us hunters."

"I take it you know the leader in Denver." He'd bet the man did.

"Jake Sutter. He just got out of the hospital. Got put there thanks to Martelli's men."

"Inform him of what has happened and that Cira Landon is safe."

"Safe is a relative term, depending on your viewpoint."

"I will not debate it with you."

"Probably a good thing." Lance moved to leave, relaxing his posture.

"Tell me," Isaac pushed. "All those missions you undertook, before you joined the hunters, did you ever save anyone?"

"Rarely."

"I see." He paused before speaking. "I trust our arrangement will continue."

"Better than what went on a hundred years ago." He glared at Isaac. "We've kept our agreement despite what happened to Jake."

"Which has been kept by us for a hundred years," Isaac returned. He knew well the agreement made. No new vampires and the hunters would stop tracking and killing them. A few exceptions had been made in situations that could not be avoided. "The threat to Cira's life made the outcome unavoidable."

"If you say so."

"Bertram did not make the decision lightly."

"How's she taking it?"

"Not as well as we had hoped."

The human smirked. "Could have told you that."

"You'll make the call to Jake."

"Already said I would." He vanished out the door.

Isaac shook his head, never sure how to take the man. In some ways, if he were to choose it, Lance would make a very good vampire.

Chapter 9
Walk in the Park

I wanted to go home for the past five days. Oh, being in Boston wasn't so bad and I certainly enjoyed the roof top view I had of the city and the bay. Bertram's home had proved to be in the Mission Hills district. Lots of historic houses located there. To me, his was more like a museum than a place to live. Antique furniture, ornate drapery and pictures I'd bet had been painted by some of the old masters.

"Enjoying the view?" my husband asked as he joined me, putting his arm around my waist.

"I'd always intended to come back," I answered pretty sure I'd already told him that. Long ago, when I'd moved away, I had promised myself I'd return. Funny how life gets in the way and pushes you in directions you hadn't expected. "And yes. I hadn't realized how much I missed the ocean."

"We can take the T for a walk in Waterfront Park if you'd like. It's a beautiful day."

Today was one of those rare warm autumn days. The leaves shimmered in tones of yellow, orange and red. Wouldn't be too much longer before the snow came and ended fall's beauty.

With a nod I allowed myself to lean against him. He drew me closer, kissing my temple. I sensed how difficult it was for him to resist what he really wanted to do. His desire seeped through, and I had a hard time shielding. Funny, the one thing I hadn't expected was for my empathic abilities to actually get stronger.

"Am I causing you discomfort?" He didn't miss my motion to pull away even as his arms tightened around me.

"Not physically." I liked being held. I just couldn't handle his emotions.

"I can't help how I feel about you." He sounded bitter. "I am your husband."

With a sigh, I pulled away, regretting what I had denied him. Bertram released me. How many times had we said the same things to each other over the past few days? "I'd love to take a walk."

"We can do that." He headed back inside. "Meet me by the door."

Taking a final look at the gorgeous view, I headed inside, ignoring the white walls covered in artwork I really didn't care for. Never ceased to amaze me what people thought good art was.

Back in my room I grabbed a sweater and headed down to the lower level. Bertram stood by the door, looking relaxed and casual. He had jeans on, and a long-sleeved shirt, wearing a Harvard hoodie. I wore jeans and a blue top as I tossed my white cardigan over my shoulders.

"Ready?" he smiled and extended his hand.

"Ready," I agreed, entwining my fingers with his. I pointed at his hoodie. "You go to school there?"

My husband chuckled. "A long time ago." He led me outside, turning on the security system before we walked to our local station.

Riding the T can be an adventure in and of itself. Long cars with seats crammed full of people from all walks of life, students in casual dress, businesspeople in their suits, various outfits from other countries who for one reason or another had resettled in the city.

My sense of smell had increased, and I smelled spicy foods, dirty bodies and others I couldn't quite identify. I covered my nose with my hand to keep them out.

"It'll get better," Bertram promised.

I hoped he was right.

We sat near the back, my husband watching the inhabitants with keen interest, a sign I'd learned meant he's hunting. No doubt he'd feed while on our outing.

Finally reaching our stop, we left the crowded car and walked toward Faneuil Hall Marketplace. I loved wandering through there when I'd lived in Boston before. Always found the most unique shops and interesting food. A mix of baked goods, pizza, and others filled the damp air.

Passing it we continued on until we reached my favorite park. Yellowed grass and trees full of color all around us. I took a deep breath of brine filled air. Reaching the edge with the bay beyond, I placed my hand on the black post connected to its partners by a long chain of the same shade.

Further out boats floated on the water with long buildings on either side filled with shops and docks. People drifted past us, their hushed whispers like loud sirens and I wanted to put my fingers in my ears to make it stop.

Bertram must have sensed how I felt. "Do you want to leave?"

I shook my head. "This is my favorite place in the entire city."

His fingers found mine and he squeezed gently. "I know you want to go home."

"I've made no secret of it."

"I'd like you to..."

"To what?" I snapped. "Stay?"

"Yes." Silence hung between us and from his expression I wished I hadn't been so short with him.

"You can't force me to be your wife if I don't..." *What? Don't want to be? Who was I kidding? I'd wondered what it would be like to make love with him when I'd found him in my bed during the convention.*

"If you don't want to be," he finished for me, his tone bitter.

I sighed, knowing I was making a mess of things. "That's not what I mean."

"Then what do you mean?" He definitely needed to feed. I could tell by how easily he got cranky.

"I need time at home." I had to sort out so many details and give both my cats a lap.

"Without me." He let go of my hand and moved to a few feet away, the breeze playing with his light reddish-brown hair.

"I just need to think." *Really?* That sounded lame even to me.

His eyes flashed red before returning to their normal color. "You agreed."

"Like I had a choice." Stay human and become a prize in a fight. Become a vampire and I gained certain rights. "I'm sorry." My eyes drifted out to gaze at the far horizon seeming endless between the water and the sky.

"At least consider the possibility." He returned to my side. "Do what you must in Denver, but return here and share my home with me." His fingers brushed my cheek. I could feel his love and berated myself for what I was doing.

"Share your home?"

"You've seen the size of it. I can convert one entire floor for your comfort. Please," he pleaded. "Please, at least consider it."

Consider it? Part of me wanted to be with him, the other to run as far away as possible. I had no idea which one would win.

~ * ~

His eyes caught a promising meal and much as he hated to leave Cira's side, he needed blood. "I'll back in a few minutes."

She nodded, her gaze never leaving whatever far point held her attention. He watched the breeze lift her dark brown hair and she absently reached up to put the errant strand back in place.

Stepping away, although it hurt him to do so, he reached the side of the young street woman he'd selected. With an easy winning smile and moment of contact with his eyes, he lured her into the shadows, took some of her blood, and left her with a twenty in her pocket for a meal he had no doubt she needed.

Back on the brick covered path, he stopped to watch his bride. She stood there hugging herself as if the breeze held a chill. It probably did. Temperatures still affected those just made and would for at least the first ten years of their existence. After that even he had to remember to wear a coat with snow on the ground and artic blasts.

"Feel better?" Cira faced him when he returned.

"Much." He dared to pull her to him and kiss her. Cira didn't fight him. Instead she relaxed. When he released her, she sighed and gazed at him with such love in her gray eyes.

"You really want me to move in with you?"

"You know I do."

"I'll consider it." She rested her head against his shoulder. He guessed he was perhaps three or four inches taller than her.

"That's all I ask."

"I have matters to settle in Denver, like selling my house, moving, and hoping my cats…" she stopped. "How are my cats?"

"They're fine. I made certain they were well cared for."

She shook her head. "I can't believe I didn't think about it until now."

"There has been a great deal going on." He enjoyed having her body pressed against him. Of course, it made him uncomfortable in another way and hoped she didn't move for a few moments.

Cira giggled. "Should I be flattered?"

Seemed she had noticed. "You should."

"I'm still not ready."

"When you are, come to me." He kissed her again. "I have something for you."

"I noticed," she teased.

"Wench," he accused, laughing at her teasing. His fingers fumbled in his pants pocket, pulling out the black box he'd put there.

She gasped as he opened it. Resting in the white velvet sat a wedding ring. He took it out and slipped it on her finger. The simple silver band had been set with a blue sapphire and two emeralds on either side.

"I don't know what to say," she murmured, staring at the ring.

"You don't have to say anything." He hoped she liked it.

"Makes our marriage more real." She frowned. "No paperwork was signed."

"I meet with my attorney tomorrow."

"Attorney?"

"He's like us and understands the complexities of our traditions and customs."

"Handy."

"You have no idea." Travis Hammer had represented him for the past hundred years.

"Do you mind if I leave tomorrow?"

"The day after would be better. I need you to come with me. There are documents that require your signature."

"Of course there are." Her tone sounded like it was obvious.

"After that, I'll have my pilot fly you back to Denver." He wanted to ask to go with her, yet knew she needed to complete her task alone. Not to mention he'd have his hands full dismantling Martelli's empire after he'd gone through the paperwork. He suspected he'd be traveling more than he wanted.

"Might take a couple of months. This is not a good time of year to sell."

"Take whatever time you need. I have to renovate the third floor for you and am not quite certain how long it might take." He put his arm around her and they walked back through the park. Bertram could see why she loved it. The overhead white trellis must be beautiful in the spring when the vines encircled it. "If you need anything specific, please let me know."

"I can do that." She chewed on her lower lip. "Are we going to call each other and keep in touch?"

Bertram smiled. "Of course." He felt her body relax. "I will be a good husband."

"I'm going to be difficult."

"Given what you've told me of your ex, Paul—" He felt angry at how the man had treated Cira. "I can be patient."

~ * ~

"How you feeling, Jake?" Lance asked, watching his kids tumble over each other in the small back yard, the smell of his wife's clam chowder filling his nose. He sat down on the low brick wall separating the lawn from the driveway.

"Better. Did I hear correctly? Martelli is dead?"

"Yep. Got his head taken."

"Any idea which vamp stepped in and took power?"

"I know who's going to dismantle it. Dr. Hoel."

"That's good to hear. We had two teens disappear with rare blood types."

"Hopefully, they make it home." The odds were slim, but Lance wanted to hold out hope to Jake.

"Hopefully", the other agreed. "Thanks for the update. What happened with Cira Landon?"

"She's one of them. No choice according to the Elders."

"Does it violate our agreement?"

"Not technically. I understood the situation and conceded the point. Happens."

"Take your word for it."

"How'd you get alerted?"

"Oh, her ex. Shit. I have to figure out what to tell him."

"As little as possible."

"Yeah. Don't want some amateur messing things up and the whole conflict gets kicked up again."

"Agreed. None of us want that." He watched his kids knowing they and his wife would be the first victims if it did. The vamps always took out the families first.

"I'll find a way. Thanks for the heads up."

"No problem. Be safe."

"You too."

He hung up and almost got knocked over when his kids tackled him. Laughing, he joined in their game, enjoying the moment, hoping the day never came when he'd have to stand by their coffins and bury them.

Chapter 10
Marriage License

Attorney's offices, not matter where they were, always look the same. An impressive wood desk the lawyer sat behind, a wall full of framed degrees, and another filled with shelved legal books. The man, or rather vampire, stood up when we entered, extending his hand, which Bertram shook.

Travis Hammer reminded me briefly of pictures I'd seen of John Adams back in the day when being a lawyer hadn't been a respectable profession. His dark hair looked a bit poufy and his sharp chocolate eyes missed nothing. He wore a tailored modern charcoal suit over his slightly pudgy body with a white shirt and a striped tie.

"Bertram, how kind of you to pay me a visit," Travis greeted, gesturing for us to be seated.

"Good to see you as well, Travis." Bertram sat and I took the chair next to him. "This is my wife Cira Landon."

I gave him a smile. He returned it.

"About time you took a bride." Travis sat back in his chair. I heard it squeak. "But a blood bride? What were you thinking?"

"Given the circumstances, it was the only choice."

"Speaking of which," he reached over and retrieved a thick file. "I received this from Martelli's attorney this morning." He pushed the documents across the desk.

Bertram took it, glancing through some of the documents. His face took on a look of surprise. "I had no idea his holdings had grown this massive."

"Rivals yours," Travis said with a grin.

Upon hearing that, I asked my husband. "In what way?"

Absently, still looking at Martelli's file, he answered. "I have two houses in London, one in Paris, several here in the states including Boston, Seattle and San Francisco, an apartment in Tokyo and Dubai."

"He owns a ranch in Kentucky where he raises and races horses," Travis filled in. "Plus a vineyard in Napa Valley and one in

France. His brands do very well. Plus…"

"I haven't had the opportunity to share with my wife," Bertram interrupted. "The number of holdings I own or my various business interests."

Travis winked at me. "He's just being modest."

"She didn't agree to marry me for my wealth."

"I suppose she did for your good looks and skill in bed?" Travis seemed to enjoy teasing my husband and probably with their long history, it had been going on for a long time.

My eyes darted down, concentrating on my hands resting on my purple skirt. I suspect my face had turned a lovely shade of red. I had no idea what Bertram was like in bed and had to admit I wanted to.

"You're embarrassing my wife," my husband chastised Travis.

"My apologies. Speaking of which," he opened another file. "I have some legal documents for you both to sign to make your marriage legal in the state of Massachusetts."

Putting Martelli's file aside, my husband accepted the documents, signed them and handed them to me. I hesitated before adding my name noting the Rosen's had signed already as witnesses and another name I didn't recognize.

"Who's this?" I asked, pointing at the name. We had no official ceremony and yet someone had signed the spot.

"Judge who owes me a favor," Travis explained, as he took the license back. "I'll get these filed for you."

"I appreciate it," Bertram said with a smile in my direction.

"You're going to have a huge job ahead of you. Martelli has been putting his empire together for at least a century. May take as long, if not more, to dismantle it."

"I know it will be a challenge."

The direction of their conversation bothered me. Why was this important to Bertram?

"I'll have a messenger deliver a copy of the files later this afternoon."

"Good enough." Bertram rose and two men shook hands again.

"It's nice to meet you, Cira," Travis said. "We've been waiting for Bertram to take a bride for quite some time."

"I'm not sure how to take that," I returned.

"As a compliment, my dear."

My husband took my arm and escorted me out of the office. While waiting for the elevator I asked, "How long has he been," I couldn't say the word.

"Oh, he was turned by his cousin Deborah Adams Metcalf."

"You mean the Elder I met at Rachel's and Isaac's?"

"The very same."

"Wait did you say Adams?"

He grinned and nodded.

"Then that is…" my mind put the pieces together. The man who was my husband's attorney was the second president of the United States!

"The very same," he agreed. The elevator arrived and we rode down to ground floor, my mind still trying to process the ramifications.

"He doesn't use his real name," Bertram shared. "Who would believe him?"

"You have a point." We crossed the street to the T station. "Are you?"

"That is my secret, dear one." His eyes sparkled. "That I may or not share with you."

~ * ~

They met at a coffee shop. One of those national chains Jake never really cared for, yet everyone frequented. He took a chair in the back and watched for the man who had contacted him originally. Sipping his black coffee, the watched patrons come and go.

When the door opened again, the man noticed him, nodded and ordered a drink before sitting down. "Well?"

"All I can tell you is she's in Boston somewhere."

"Yeah, but is she safe?"

"Last I heard she was well." No need to tell him the full truth. He didn't need this man going rogue and getting a bunch of innocents killed. That's why they'd made the agreement with the vamps to begin with, too much bloodshed on both sides.

"You're sure she's safe?" His expression said he didn't believe a word he'd been told.

"Positive. We have people everywhere. I verified it myself." He took another drink, watching the other very carefully. "Just stay out of this and let us handle it. No need to get yourself killed."

"I'm not afraid." His bravado felt fake.

"You should be." He had to make his warning very clear. "They're very dangerous."

"Once you find her, you'll let me know."

"Soon as we know anything," he promised despite knowing not a word would be said.

"I'll keep in contact."

"You do that." He took a drink again.

With a huff, the man left, his body language expressing his fury far better than his expression or words. He watched the other drive out of the parking lot, almost running over two people.

The guy was dangerous. They'd need to watch him.

~ * ~

The messenger arrived at about two. Bertram accepted the documents and tipped the college aged youth generously. The kid grinned. "Thanks."

"You're welcome."

He closed the door and took the file to his office located at the back of the house, with a window facing a small garden. Given the time of year, most of the plants had gone dormant or died. Many would return in the spring as a wild colorful mix.

A light tap sounded on his door, which he'd left open. He looked up and gave Cira a smile. "Come in," he invited.

She hesitated. "I hope I'm not interrupting."

"You are never an interruption."

She came in and went to the window looking out. "I'll bet this is pretty when everything is in bloom."

"It is." He waited for her to decide to share why she'd come.

Her hands twisted nervously. "You're sure I'm not disturbing you?"

"You aren't." It concerned him she thought so. "Why do you ask?"

With a sigh she faced him. "I'm sorry. My ex always yelled at me if I went into his office to talk with him. Said he was busy, and I should leave him alone."

More evidence of the mistreatment she'd received from a man who supposedly loved her. "Cira," he got up and lightly traced his finger across her cheek. "I am not him. You are always welcome to speak with me at any time."

She looked uncertain.

He dared to kiss her, enjoying the feel of her lips. "Now, tell me why you have come."

"I," she looked down. "I'll be leaving tomorrow and have no idea when I'll be back."

"My jet is standing by." He missed her already and she hadn't left yet.

"You made me a promise."

Bertram waited, unsure what she wanted to say.

"It's going to be awhile before we're together again and…" Her hand gently touched his face, her eyes reflecting her uncertainty. "I would like…" she stopped. She glanced down, her voice very quiet. "To make love before I leave."

He blinked caught by surprise. "Are you sure?"

Cira nodded, looking like a frightened rabbit ready to flee.

Taking her into his arms, he kissed her, gently at first, allowing her time to adjust to his passion. His hands passed over her clothes, feeling her body under the fabric.

His office definitely was not the place to make love to his wife. Sweeping her up in his arms, he carried her up the stairs to his bedroom, placing her on the bed, his eager fingers taking off her top, while his mouth explored her small and firm breasts.

~ * ~

I moaned with pleasure, my hands helping Bertram shed his shirt, my fingers running across his hairy chest, lingering on the scar he would carry, a reminder of his marriage oath to me.

He caught my hand and kissed it before undressing me until I lay naked before him. His glowing golden-brown eyes took a moment to gaze at my body. "You are glorious," he breathed, his lips claiming mine before his mouth moved slowly down, exploring I swear every inch of me!

His attention caused my body to awake in ways I had never experienced while his musky scent filled my nose. I knew I wanted him and my fingers worked at his pants zipper, which would not budge.

He stopped me. "Let me do that. It will be easier." Quickly he removed the last of his clothing.

Have to admit he had a nice body, too bad I hadn't paid attention on our wedding night. I could feel a slight chill as I touched him. Vampires are warmest just after they've fed, which fades after a few hours.

"You always smell like vanilla," he whispered, nuzzling my neck, sending a pleasant tingling through my body.

I gasped at the sensations he aroused in me. Making love with my ex had always been fun, but never this intense.

"Please," I begged.

"What do you want?" he teased. I felt his hardness pressing against the interior of my thigh. His desire for me slipped past my shield, causing me to feel his pleasure and need.

"Take me," I pleaded.

My husband lifted his head, his eyes gazing at me. "Your eyes are glowing."

"So are yours," I returned. "Stop teasing me."

"Gladly," he agreed sliding inside, moving slowly as we finally joined as husband and wife.

~ * ~

"Wow," Cira breathed, kissing him.

He turned on his side, taking her with him. "You are pleased."

"Extremely." Her fingers ran down his chest. "If I were a cat I'd be purring. Loudly."

Her comment made him laugh. "If you were a cat..."

"Oh, hush." She placed her finger on his lips. "Now I don't want to leave."

"Then don't."

"If I'm to come here to live with you, I need to."

"Then wait a few days." He couldn't wait to touch her again. "I want to show you the blueprints and plans I have for the third floor."

"At least you won't have to put in a spare bedroom. Looks like I'll be sharing yours."

"Ours," he corrected. Kissing her, he felt his excitement grow. Vampires had much better stamina than human men, one fact Isaac had shared. Bertram intended to make love to his wife until they both lay completely sated and exhausted.

Chapter 11

Journey

"I hate to leave," I told Bertram as we stood at the ramp leading up to the open jet door, the faint smell of fuel drifting on the air.

"We have discussed this." His finger trailed slowly down my cheek and along my neck. I shivered enjoying the sensation. "You need to close out your life there."

"Only a few days ago I couldn't wait to leave." I looked into his golden-brown eyes.

"Amazing what can change in such a short time." He kissed me, holding me tightly in his arms. I sensed his strong desire for me and him fighting to control it. He released me; his eyes glowing. "I will miss you."

"Me too." I forced myself to climb the ramp, stopping at the top to give him a quick wave before I entered the plane. Inside I found a couple of couches, a few chairs and a small desk area. Made perfect sense. He used the plane for business purposes.

Taking a seat on the light gold couch, I fastened the belt while an attendant outside closed the door. Minutes later the pilot announced, "We're taxing for takeoff Mrs. Hoel. Please make sure you're buckled in."

I hadn't actually changed my last name to my husband's, but didn't bother trying to correct him. Settling back, I watched through the window as the plane rose in the sky, feeling the familiar pressure changes as we left the ground for the sky.

Once in the air, I moved to the desk, and opened my laptop. Since I had time, I might as well get some writing done. I had a deadline for my next book and with all my life changes, I'd almost forgotten. Plunging myself into my characters' world, I started when the pilot announced we'd be landing in thirty minutes. I saved my work and backed it up, before putting my laptop away and buckling in for landing.

We landed not at DIA, but a smaller airfield in Centennial. The pilot left the cockpit, giving me a polite nod as he opened the door. "They'll be putting the ramp in place momentarily, Mrs. Hoel."

"Thank you."

"My pleasure." He waited until I had disembarked. My luggage had been unloaded and put into the back of a waiting limo.

The driver opened the door. "Let's get you out the sunlight. It's more direct here."

I understood all about the altitude. In the Mile Hi City I had the risk of burning as a new vampire. One I did not face at or below sea level. Bertram had explained the danger to me before I left. One of those rare exceptions to sunlight exposure. I slid into the back and the door was shut.

"Where to, Mrs. Hoel?" the driver asked from the front seat.

I gave him the address and he pulled out onto the streets where I had lived many years, my feelings mixed about being back. Probably because I knew my home was now in Boston with my husband. Part of me had put down roots in Colorado and I knew how painful it would be to pull them loose.

About twenty minutes later, we pulled up in front of my home. While I was away, it must have snowed. Patches lingered on the grass and bushes. A small creek ran along the road and sidewalk, deep enough to hide the bottom of the tires for those who had parked on the street.

Leaving the limo, the driver took my luggage to the door, touched his hat goodbye and left me. My husband had found my spare keys and made certain I had one so I could enter my home. Unlocking the door, two sets of yellow eyes greeted me. From the scattered toys I assumed I must have interrupted their play.

"Hi Anghel, Sophie." Both cats ignored me, as I suspected they would. After all, I had left them alone for several weeks. Pulling my luggage inside, I looked over my home. The rooms looked intact and my fur babies had plenty of water and food. The cat sitter must have taken very good care of them.

On the ledge separating my kitchen from my dining room, the latter of which I used as an office instead, I found a note.

Hi,

Just wanted to let you know I took very good care of your cats. Dr. Hoel let me know you were coming home today. I left the key next to my note. If you have any questions or concerns, please feel free to give me call.

Oh, and welcome to the family.

June

She included her number. My husband told me the fee had been covered, but not the details. I sensed he hadn't told me the full truth and I hadn't pushed. Being over two hundred, I suspected he had many secrets he might never share.

Sinking down on my dark blue recliner, the thought of having to pack up my life and move across country felt overwhelming. Granted, my husband would cover the cost. He'd given me access to his bank account, a huge sign of trust. I'd do my best not to abuse it.

First step, make a list of what I needed to do, which would include calling my realtor. I'd decided it would be easier to pack up and let the house be shown empty. After all, most of the paperwork could be handled via email.

I put my head in my hands. So many decisions to be made and I couldn't make them without some rest. Funny to think vampires needed at least six hours of sleep, if you call the twilight place we enter that.

Rising I made my way upstairs, took a quick shower and crawled into my bed. I missed Bertram being there beside me. The body pillow I snuggled against proved a poor substitute although I enjoyed the two little furred bodies cuddling along my back and legs, washing themselves and purring. They must have forgiven me.

Closing my eyes, I traveled into the twilight, a sense of unease haunting me and faintly I heard Martelli's echoing laugh.

Chapter 12

Killing Spree

Bertram stared at Isaac's message on his computer screen.

Bertram,

Confirmed vampire death in Denver. Dr. Alice Dugger, a researcher at University Hospital and part of the volunteer staff at our emergency clinic, was found beheaded in her Lonetree home.

I will be meeting with Lance in two hours. Please attend.

Isaac

The message had been sent fifteen minutes ago. Part of him felt relieved the victim hadn't been Dr. Malik. He began to worry. Cira had returned to Denver ten days ago. Would she be next on the killer's list?

Another thought entered his mind. Had the hunters decided him taking Cira as his blood bride broke their long-term agreement and caused them to resume the hunt? He hoped not.

He called for his car. When it arrived, he left making certain he locked the door and set his security system. The ride took a bit longer due to traffic, causing his nerves to be on edge when they finally arrived at Isaac and Rachel's home.

"Should I wait, sir?" his driver asked.

"I'm not certain how long this may take. Just wait for my call."

"I'll be standing by."

Getting out, Bertram hurried to the door. Rachel opened it for him before he even knocked. "They're in the living room," she told him, closing the heavy oak behind him before following.

All the Elders were in attendance along with a very nervous human, in jeans and a long-sleeved shirt, who tried to look confident. Isaac had been speaking with him as Bertram and Rachel entered.

"Suppose you share with the Elders what you just told me," Isaac instructed, sitting on the couch.

"Fine," the other bit out. "Look, the hunters aren't responsible for Dr. Duggar's death."

"Then who is?" Deborah Metcalf demanded, in her normal brown dress.

"Probably a rogue." He shifted his weight from one foot to another. Bertram got the impression the man had probably once served in the military.

"You're sure this is not retribution for me taking Cira as a blood bride?" Bertram had to know.

"The situation has been explained to me. Besides," he crossed his arms over his black top. "We built safeguards into the agreement. Taking a blood bride being one of them and a few others, like killing a human if they killed one of you."

A chilling suspicion crawled into his thoughts. "What about Cira's ex, Paul?"

"I'll be talking to Jake and have him check. I know the guy wasn't happy we didn't do more when she disappeared." He rubbed his forehead. "Jake told him later she was fine. He said the guy has a nasty temper and almost hurt several people."

"A rogue." Isaac shook his head, looking older than normal. "Not often one of them surfaces."

"He has to be put down." Jacob's red eyes reflected his anger.

"If we can prove it's Cira's ex." Lance met the other's gaze. "I won't sanction the killing otherwise."

Jacob nodded his agreement. They all knew if they killed a human who later proved to be innocent, the agreement would be broken, and the hunters would come after them again.

"Done." Isaac looked around the room. "We all know the conditions."

"I'll contact Jake as soon as this meeting is over," Lance assured them. "I'll keep you updated on what I find out."

"In the meantime, the vampires in Denver need to be warned." Isaac's sympathetic eyes caught Bertram's.

"Fine. Do what you have to." Lance walked through the room and they all heard the front door slam.

"He's frightened," Naomi said, sitting next to her husband.

"He has reason to be," Isaac agreed. "He has a family."

Bertram hated the implication and the loss of young innocent lives. If this exploded into a war between the hunters and vampires, how many would die before they completely destroyed each other. The numbers would be staggering.

The Elders broke into smaller groups, their fear evident by their expressions and hushed voices. Isaac motioned for Bertram to join him and Rachel.

"Cira's in Denver isn't she?" Rachel asked, her hand smoothing her gingham skirt.

"She is and probably has no idea of the danger she's in. If her ex, Paul, is responsible, she's a target." He couldn't keep his worry out of his voice.

"Weren't you about to leave for Atlanta, to end the rare blood trafficking trade there?" Isaac inquired, standing up.

"In a few days." He wasn't so certain he should go. Not if his bride's life might be in danger.

"For now we know very little." Isaac lightly touched his shoulder. "Take your jet, do what you planned. Call your wife and let her know to be careful."

"I hate leaving her alone to face this." If she suffered the same fate as Dr. Duggar, he couldn't be held responsible for his actions.

"Bertram," Rachel's soft voice broke through his worry. "Her best defense is to be aware."

"I'll call her in a few minutes. Is Denver the only place we've had a loss?"

"It is," Isaac confirmed. "Should that change, I'll let you know. Now, go save innocent lives as you planned and shut down Martelli's southern trafficking ring."

Deborah joined them, her long skirts whispering across the floor. "Isaac is correct."

"I'd feel better if I were with her." Bertram clenched his hand.

"As a good husband should be." She smiled and he could see the family resemblance with his old friend Travis. "My cousin sensed the same thing I did. Cira is our blood descendant."

Bertram started, her meaning dawning on him. "Then I definitely should go to her."

"No." Deborah shook her head. "Go save the innocents stolen from their homes. No need to worry about Cira." An unreadable expression crossed her face. "She's my concern."

Not sure how to take her words, he nodded. "If you'll excuse me."

Isaac waved him away while the three Elders conversed. Going into the kitchen, he called his wife, impatient when the phone went straight to voice mail. He waited a few minutes and called again. This time she answered, "Hi Bertram."

Relieved he sat down at the table feeling like his legs wouldn't support his weight. "You're all right."

"Of course I am. Bertram, is something wrong?"

Quickly he filled her in on what had happened in Denver. He heard her frightened gasp. "Do you want me to come back to Boston?"

"Not unless you've completed your packing."

"I'm almost there. I have a meeting with my realtor today. That could take a couple of hours."

"Just be careful and observant."

"Promise. Get down from there! Sorry, Sophie decided to play king of the mountain on a stack of boxes filled with breakables."

"Sounds like you have your hands full"

"I do. How are the renovations going?"

"They'll be completed in a couple of days." He pushed the workmen to finish quickly so the renovations would be done by the time she came home.

"Good. The moving truck will be here in a week."

"Given the situation, I don't want you driving cross country. I'll send the jet for you and the cats."

"That'll work. I'll go ahead and sell my car. I have a couple of interested buyers anyway." She laughed. "Besides, having a car in Boston is kind of pointless."

He chuckled. "I agree."

"Returning by jet will make it easier on me and my fur babies. I wasn't looking forward to hearing them yowl the entire way."

"Then it is settled." He paused, trying to decide how to tell her. "I'll be in Atlanta when you return."

"Oh." He heard her disappointment.

"It's my first step in putting an end to Martelli's criminal activities."

"I still don't approve." She sounded both worried and angry.

"I'll be fine," he tried to reassure her again. They'd discussed what he wanted to do many times.

She sighed. "Just be careful."

"I promise I will."

"At some point, I want to hear what happened between you and Martelli."

"One day." He still hadn't decided if she really needed to

know.

"Sooner is better than later." Her tone let him know there would be no argument about it. "Maybe it will help me understand why you're trying to undo everything he did."

"We will sit down together and I will tell you the whole story." He heard himself say.

"I'll hold you to your promise." Yowls and screeches in the background sounded ominous. "I have to go, love."

"So I hear. I love you."

"Love you too. I'll be home soon."

"Looking forward to seeing you soon." He ended the call, feeling as if a part of his heart was missing. At least she hadn't argued too much with him. His notified his driver and headed home to confirm the renovations would be done in time for his wife's arrival.

~ * ~

His children slept peacefully and Lance hoped they would continue to do so. His wife had gone to the local bar to hang with her friends for the night. She'd told him she needed a break, for him to watch the kids, and promised to be back by midnight. He did a quick check on all the doors and windows before settling in their living room with a good book.

A ringing brought him out of the world he had dived into and he answered annoyed at the interruption. "Yes?"

"Lance, it's Jake."

His full attention diverted to the call. "Jake, what is going on?"

"I can confirm the rogue is Cira Landon's ex, Paul. We arrived minutes after he burned poor June to death."

"Wait, wasn't she a half-blood?" Isaac would be furious to hear the fate of his granddaughter. Lance dreaded having to tell him, if he didn't already know.

"Yeah. One of the few."

"You can confirm it was Mrs. Hoel's ex, Paul?"

"Saw him myself and I recognized his car. Got the plate memorized."

"All right." Lance took a deep breath before doing what he had to for the protection of everyone. "Paul's death is sanctioned. Doesn't matter if he's killed by a hunter or a vamp."

"Understood."

"And Jake, put a watch on Cira Landon Hoel. He may not know she's a vamp yet, but I'd bet she's his endgame."

"Like they say on those TV shows," Jake shot back, trying to lighten Lance's dark mood.

"As they say," Lance agreed, appreciating the gesture. He'd have a long night since an official proclamation needed to be made and delivered to both hunters and vampires. "I'll see if I can find out when Mrs. Hoel is leaving. With any luck it will be soon."

"Who's gonna tell the Elders about June?"

"That's my job." He dreaded his task and Isaac Rosen's reaction.

"I don't pity you. Good luck." Jake hung up.

Lance sat there for several minutes before calling Isaac to tell him about June. The Elder took the news more calmly than expected, probably because they knew who was responsible.

"Kill him," Isaac said, his voice dripping with angry grief. "Or we will."

"Understood." Lance hung up and went to look at his children, sleeping peacefully, and innocent, unaware of the dangerous supernatural world that could consume them. He wanted to keep them that way for as long as possible. The door opened and his wife entered. Seeing his expression she put her arms around him and said, "It's bad."

"Very. Pack up the kids and take them to your parents in the morning. Don't come back until I tell you."

"I will." She kissed him. "I love you."

"I love you too."

Chapter 13
Moving

Every call from my husband during the last six days filled me with dread. Seven dead vampires either beheaded or burned, including a half-blood. I had to ask what they were since I hadn't heard the word before. Evidently, they are children of a vampire and a human. In extremely rare instances, either a vampire male can impregnate a human woman or a human man can do the same with a vampire woman. June was one of those exceptions and although I'd never met her, I mourned her loss. She'd done such a good job caring for my fur babies.

In two days, my husband's jet would arrive at Centennial airport to take me back to Boston. I wouldn't board until every item I owned got packed on the truck and I did a final walkthrough to make certain every closet and cupboard was empty. At that time, I'd let the drivers start their journey to our home in Boston.

My realtor already had a key to the house and would list my home. Once it sold I would bank the profit in an account separate from my husband's. Bertram hadn't liked my decision when I'd told him. I had explained my reasons and he'd reluctantly agreed to them. I wanted money of my own and at least a sense of independence.

The hunters had taken up residence near my home. They changed daily, so I never knew who would be sitting in what car watching.

I had to admit I felt unsafe, even with the windows and doors locked. My ex did repair work and I suspected he could break into my home anytime he wanted. Bertram seemed to think I was in danger and the hunters must have agreed given their continued presence.

Walking across the carpet, looking around at empty walls and piled boxes, I felt nostalgic about my townhouse. It had been my home after Paul had walked out on me. Oh, he'd given me the marital residence, with unrealistic expectations I would keep the place so he'd have a free place to store his stuff. *Yeah, right.*

I wanted and deserved a place of my own. One which didn't remind me every day about my failed marriage and the abuse I'd suffered.

A clean fresh start is what I had needed.

Now, I was starting over again with a man who loved me and assured me daily he supported my goals. Such a nice change, although I had to wonder if he was a little too good to be true. I hadn't seen a weakness in him as he appeared always so strong and confident. Everyone had a vulnerable point. I probably hadn't discovered his yet.

Sophie and Anghel sat on the stairs, glaring down at me for disrupting their home. Both of their heads jerked up and they fled when the doorbell rang.

Who could that be?

Once glance outside and I didn't want to answer. Standing there on my concrete porch stood Paul wearing jeans and a sweater. Cautiously I opened the door, latching the screen door. "What do you want?" He smelled of spicy cologne.

"Can I come in?" He no doubt expected me to open the door.

"No." My eyes darted to the car where the hunter sat, daring to hope they'd interfere.

"Why not?" He glared at me. "Is he here?"

"Who?" Like I didn't know. My ex's anger burned so strongly I snapped my shield in place. He still burned through.

"That damned vampire!" he yelled.

"To whom are you referring?" I returned calmly. If I yelled back, it would make him even more angry.

"That fake scientist who was at the con. Dr. Bertram Hoel!" He grabbed the screen door trying to open it. I heard it rattle.

"That's none of your business. Now leave before I call the police." I started to close the door.

"Did he turn you?" I felt no concern from him.

"You're talking nonsense. Now go away." I shut the door and locked it. He rang the doorbell again and again. I ignored him, continuing to pack another box to keep my mind off his annoying presence.

I heard sirens and looked out the patio door. A police car pulled up and an officer jumped out slowly approaching. Paul howled like a wounded animal and fled. So, the hunter had called them for me.

The cop got back into his car and chased my ex, who tried to outrun him on foot. They disappeared around the corner. I stepped outside and waved my thanks. The hunter nodded.

Back inside, I sat down and started to shake. I fumbled for my phone and called Bertram. I desperately needed to his reassurance. It went straight to voice mail.

"Paul came for me," my voice shook, as tears streamed down my face. "Bertram, he came for me."

Chapter 14
Night Before

Midnight and the city below him, for the fortunate humans, slept. Bertram gazed out the hotel window deciding most metropolis views pretty much seemed the same: lights, tall buildings and the sound of traffic drifting up. Stepping away, he knew he'd need to rest. Tomorrow would be a busy day.

At stake, the lives of two dozen young people being delivered to the Laroe estate. A special order placed by one of the oldest vampire families, who, despite not being Elders, held great influence not just over Atlanta, but much of the south.

Bertram understood the danger of what he meant to do. His life would be forfeit and no one would know what had happened. Luckily, he'd left Travis specific instructions about his estate, holdings, and bank accounts. Cira would get most of it. He suspected she might object, but since he knew their marriage had been for other reasons and not his riches, Bertram felt comfortable with his decision.

He regretted not being able to speak with his wife earlier when she'd called. The arranged meeting with the hunters could not be interrupted and with so much riding on its success, he had to wait. Curious about why she'd called, he checked the message she'd left.

"Paul came for me," she sounded very upset. "Bertram, he came for me." Then she hung up.

He stared at the phone before calling her back, praying, the worst had not happened. After several rings, she answered, sounding a bit groggy. "You have any idea what time it is?"

"I'm two hours ahead of you," he answered. "And yes."

"Sorry," she apologized. He heard movement. "I went to bed early since the movers are coming at eight."

"I won't keep you long. What happened today?"

Cira quickly shared with him the events of her ex's visit. How he'd tried to force his way in and the police arriving. "He ran off down the street around the block with the cop in pursuit. My guess is the hunter called them."

At least they were keeping their end of the bargain. "I'm sending the jet to Denver tonight. As soon as your home is loaded up and the moving truck leaves, I want you in a car and headed for the airport." His concern for her safety caused Bertram to sit down. "Please. I want you out of harm's way." He'd been told her ex was killing Denver vampires and if Paul found out about Cira, he'd kill her too.

"How soon before you come home?" she asked. At least she hadn't objected to the change of plans.

"As soon as I can." No need to explain to her the danger he faced.

"I miss you."

"And I miss you. Once I get this ring shut down, my next move will be the one in Maine."

"This is going to go on for a while isn't it?" She sounded unhappy.

"I told you it would."

"You did," Cira admitted. "Once my belongings arrive, it'll keep me busy unpacking." She didn't say them, but he heard the words anyway. 'So, I won't worry so much about you.'

"How many of my paintings are you going to move and replace?" He'd told her she could decorate anyway she wanted, but it concerned him. His artwork held great value.

"Let's talk about that when you're home." She yawned. "Right now, I'd like to get back to sleep."

"You know what I'd like to be doing to you right now?" he taunted seductively.

She groaned. "This is the wrong night for phone sex, Bertram."

"Or the right one."

"I'm going back to bed. We'll talk tomorrow. Night, Bertram." She hung up.

He shook his head and disconnected, a little disappointed she hadn't wanted to play along. No doubt it would have helped them both relax.

Before he recharged his phone, Bertram placed a call to his pilot to arrange for the jet to fly to Denver. Afterward, he stripped and crawled between the sheets, which smelled heavily of bleach, closing his eyes. Dawn would come soon and he needed his wits about him if he intended to save lives.

He just hoped his plan didn't cost him his in the process.

Chapter 15

Saying Goodbye

Moving is a nightmare. Boxes everywhere, remembering just before the mayhem started to secure my cats in the upstairs bathroom with everything they needed, movers in and out of the house all day, my belongings being packed into a huge orange truck, my neighbors dropping by to say goodbye. We're a tight knit community. I'd miss them even as they wished me well.

I did a quick check to see if my hunter protector hovered nearby. They did of course. The first guy in his beat-up jeep. A car kept driving by and I didn't recognize it. When I tried to get a good look at the driver, he or she, pulled their hat tighter and drove off. Their behavior concerned me in light of knowing a rogue vampire killer stalked us.

The truck finally got loaded by late afternoon. I did a final walkthrough, checking closets, cupboards, nooks and crannies where I may have put something. Nothing got missed. I told the movers to leave and called the driver my husband always had on call before placing one to my realtor.

"Hi Betsy," I said when she answered.

"Hi Cira, how did the move go?"

"About the way I expected. Hectic." I glanced out the window. "I have a car on the way to take me to the airport."

"You go have a fabulous life with your new husband. You deserve it." She sounded very happy for me.

"Thank you. Oh, here's my new address." I gave it to her. "Just in case there's unexpected mail or you or the new owners find anything."

"Got it," she told me. "You're going to be missed."

"I'll miss being here." I laughed tiredly. "In a way this is a good thing. I always wanted to go back to Boston. Just hadn't expected events to happen this way."

"That's the way God works. Opens doors when we least expect it."

Good thing I didn't think of myself as a damned creature like those vampire movies I've watched or else her comment would have upset me.

"We've already taken care of most of the paperwork," Betsy went on. "When I sell your place, I'll give you a call."

"Just let me know. I'll have a private jet for my use." Still hadn't gotten used to that. I normally travelled commercial airlines by coach.

"Must be nice." She didn't sound envious.

"Different." I heard a knock at the door and recognized the driver. "Have to go, my ride is here."

"Soon as we have a contract, I'll be in touch. Bye and have a safe trip."

"Thanks. Bye." I disconnected and went to the door. "Give me a few minutes to load up the cats and the items I'm taking with me."

"Take your time, Mrs. Hoel."

Getting the cats into the carriers is always a nightmare. My vet had taught me a trick. Get them by the scruff of their neck and lower them, butt first inside, then shut the door. I took them downstairs. The driver carried them to the limo. They hissed the entire way.

Gathering up my luggage, plus a few items I insisted on taking personally, I left the key with the other spares in a kitchen drawer and took one last look at my home. "Goodbye," I whispered, before locking the door and making my way to the car.

The driver had already taken the two boxes I'd packed to the limo. He took my luggage putting them in the trunk. I crawled in knowing I'd hear the cats yowl for the entire drive. "It's okay," I assured them, managing to pet both their heads with a finger through the metal wire doors, weaved like a very loose basket.

As we drove through traffic, I called my husband, which went straight to voice mail. I knew he had an important task today, so it didn't overly concern me. "Hi, Love, just wanted to let you know I'm on my way to the jet. The truck will take a few days to arrive." I glanced back and noticed the same car which had kept driving through the neighborhood earlier. "See you when you get back. I miss you. Be safe."

Sitting back in the seat, I tried not to allow my imagination to run wild. The driver simply might be going the same way. The hunters had proven excellent allies so I knew it wasn't them.

We pulled into the airport finally, the limo being waved

through the large metal gate. The car I'd noticed stopped across the street and I could see a motion like a person beating the steering wheel over and over. A chill spread through me. I knew that behavior.

Dear God! My ex, Paul, had followed me!

~ * ~

Bertram listened to his wife's message that she was headed for the jet, while the driver he'd hired drove through Atlanta, turning north toward the plantation where he'd be meeting with the Laroe's. They still grew coffee, tobacco and a few fields of cotton. They'd been southern gentry for over a hundred years and an important client of Martelli's for over seventy-five.

They liked rare blood types. Their shipment would be arriving separately, and Bertram had coordinated with the hunters to have the truck diverted. The container he'd arranged for would be full of his allies. The plan, if it worked, would put an end to the trade. He just hoped he could convince them to stop, if not, well, that's why he'd brought back up.

The car turned down a tree lined road. Peach trees of course, Georgia was famous for them. Ahead sat a Greek Revival house, painted white and surrounded by beautiful pink magnolia bushes. He could smell the fragrance even this far away. The property held several ponds, and he could see the reptilian gator heads.

A well-dressed tall man saw him coming and took the porch stairs, waiting for Bertram's arrival. The southern aristocrat nodded at him as he got out of the car. In one glance, Bertram got a measure of the man. Used to holding power, he had a handsome face, at least to the ladies. He wondered how many the vampire had wooed. What he noticed most was the cold calculating eyes and the coal black hair with a hint of gray above the ears.

"Dr. Hoel," the accented deep voice greeted. "We'd heard about the challenge." The man grinned. "I'm Jackson Laroe. I trust our shipment will be arriving shortly."

"It will." No need to tell him differently.

"Good. We've had a long and profitable relationship with Lionel Martelli. We trust that will continue."

"I'm here to negotiate."

"I like a man who's upfront." He motioned toward the house. "If you'd like to step inside, my wife has prepared some refreshments."

Southern hospitality, Bertram had experienced it many times. "Thank you." He walked with the other inside. The temperature seemed a bit cooler, not that it would make a difference to him. Jackson led him into the drawing room, the furniture very much like one would expect for a home this old. Wood and white velvet, with flowery wallpaper and a lovely hand carved fireplace.

"We've talked about updating," Mr. Laroe explained. He must have seen Bertram's interest. "But my wife is quite partial to the furniture we had made when we married." He smiled as a beautiful woman entered in an elegant long dress, her blonde hair piled attractively. She carried a silver tray with a China teapot and cups.

"Welcome to our home, Dr. Hoel," she greeted, placing the tray on a low table. "I hope you like peach tea."

"One of my favorites, Mrs. Laroe," he lied smoothly, giving her a smile.

"Most here call me Ruth." She handed him a cup. "Sugar or cream?"

"Thank you, no."

He waited until Mr. Laroe had been given his cup. The man chose a chair near the fireplace. "We hear you brought home a lovely bride."

Taking a place on the loveseat, he watched Ruth sit near her husband, sipping her tea.

"Let's just say the circumstances were unusual." He sipped the brew and tried not to make a face, not caring for the blend.

"How is she adjusting?" Mrs. Laroe asked.

"As well as can be expected." No need to tell them more. Cira should be home in a few hours. He looked forward to seeing her soon, if all went as planned.

In a distance Bertram heard the truck traveling down the road. He put down his half empty cup. "I understand your children still live here."

"Such a blessing to have them around," Ruth replied with a fond smile. "Of course, we waited until they grew up to have them join us. Our boys both claimed brides. Our daughter, sadly, hasn't found anyone worthy of her."

"I'm sure she will in time." Bertram tried not to be nervous. So far, everything had gone as planned.

Mr. Laroe nodded, putting down his cup. "We're sure she will.

I hear the truck approaching. Shall we adjourn outside and see what you've brought us?"

"Of course." Bertram rose, feeling uneasy. An odd burning started in his stomach. He tried not to show his discomfort.

The truck rumbled to a stop. Men Bertram didn't know got out and unlocked the back. Crammed inside were men and women in shackles. The handlers forced them out. Many of them blinked, trying to shade their eyes and their soiled clothes reeked.

Bertram shifted nervously as his stomach roiled and his veins burned. The shipment of humans had not been intercepted. His truck full of hunters must have either missed it or his plan had been discovered.

The southern aristocrat gave him a mocking smile. "It seems you failed, Dr. Hoel."

~ * ~

The man stormed into the coffee shop, almost knocking down a young mother trying to quiet her crying baby. He glared at them both and fixed his furious eyes on Jake, sitting at a back table calmly drinking his coffee, even while his heart hammered, knowing he had to be careful.

"Where the hell is she?" he demanded, slamming his fist down on the wooden table.

"I suggest keeping your voice down and not drawing any unnecessary attention." Jake continued to hold his cup just in case the man decided to hit the top again.

"You were there," he accused.

"Keeping watch is ninety percent of what we do."

"Did he turn her?"

"They don't tell us when they add to their number," he lied.

"Where'd she go? I saw the moving truck being loaded and I followed her to the airport."

Jake shrugged, keeping in mind how dangerous this man was. Since they'd met publicly, he couldn't take action on the death order, much as he wanted to. "We don't have that information."

"You're lying!" Every head in room turned to look in their direction.

"Keep your voice down," Jake warned again, keeping his tone level and calm. Arguing with Paul would only set him off and who knew what would happen or who might get hurt. He knew humans often proved more dangerous than vamps.

"Then get me the information I need," the man hissed, "so I can go after her." He stormed out, banging the door open, and cracking the glass.

Taking a deep breath to calm himself, he finished his coffee and left, very aware of the sympathetic stares. Once back in his jeep, he put in a call to Lance.

"What's up, Jake?" the hunter leader asked.

"Get the word out to Dr. Hoel and Isaac that Cira's ex, Paul, is trying to find out where she is and go after her."

"That's the least of our worries."

Jake started. "Why? What's wrong?"

"Got a call from our southern branch. Seems a powerful vamp family there got wind of what Dr. Hoel had planned for their blood shipment and ambushed his backup."

Jake swore colorfully. "Did they kill them all?"

"Oddly enough, they're alive. Seems the vamps were smart enough not to re-ignite the war."

"What about Dr. Hoel?"

"Unknown."

"Shit."

~ * ~

Bertram had been poisoned very cleverly by Mrs. Laroe. She'd spiked his tea. The potion wouldn't kill him, just make him very ill. So much so he'd been unable to defend himself when the master of the house and his sons had dragged him across the lawns. He'd caught the pitying looks on a few of the humans' faces before they disappeared from his view.

In the storm cellar under the main house, the sons chained Bertram, the cuffs biting painfully into his wrists and he felt the poison burn. They must have coated the manacles. The place smelled moldy and dank causing his stomach to squeeze his gut and he groaned in pain.

"Enjoy your quarters," Mr. Laroe taunted. "You're going to be here for quite some time." The vampire rubbed his hands together. "Perhaps I'll invite your lovely wife for a visit."

Cira, here? No! "Leave her out of this!"

"We'll see." The trio turned to leave. "Be a good boy."

They vanished up the stairs and slammed the double doors shut. He heard a lock slid into place and their laughter as they moved away, followed by screams. No doubt the family feasted.

At least there wasn't any annoying water dripping constantly. That would have been cliché. He did hear scurrying and figured he had rodent company. Whether mice or rats, he couldn't be sure. No light shown through. Not that it mattered. Bertram had a high tolerance and his eyes could see in the darkness.

They'd left him with his shoes, so at least his feet wouldn't be touching the grimy floor. He would have to stand. The chain, from his testing of them, had proved to not be very long. His physical position would be uncomfortable, but not too intolerable.

Except for the constant burning around his wrists. No doubt they were blistered. He'd need blood to heal the wounds. Somehow, he doubted the Laroes had any intention of feeding him.

~ * ~

The jet touched down with a jolt waking me. I'd managed to doze off after I'd let the cats out. The tabby pair had settled beside me, their purring lulling me to sleep. I could feel the plane taxiing and stayed put until it had come to a complete stop.

When it had, I wrestled Sophie and Anghel back into their carrier's despite their protests, thinking I should call for the car. I'd picked up my phone to complete the task when the captain exited.

"The Rosen's are waiting to take you home."

"Excuse me?" What in the world were Isaac and Rachel doing here?

"I got their message just as we landed, Mrs. Hoel." He opened the door. "The handlers are below to unload your luggage and other packages."

"Thank you, Captain." I watched as the stairs slid into place and kept clear of the door as the men smelling of sweat and grease, picked up my luggage and boxes, carrying them off the jet. About to pick up the carriers, the captain surprised me by taking them.

At the bottom of the stairs Isaac waited, a worried smile greeting me. *Oh, dear God, what could possibly be wrong?* I could feel his turbulent emotions.

"Hello, Isaac," I greeted, feeling uneasy.

"Welcome home, Cira." He kissed my hand. Must be an old-fashioned thing. He looked comfortable in his dark gray suit. "Rachel is waiting in the car."

My sense of dread increased as I ducked inside. The carriers sat across from me on the floor and I'm guessing everything else had been put in the trunk.

"You two want to tell me what's wrong?" I asked after Isaac took a seat beside his wife.

The pair exchanged a look. The kind when you know they'd been married for so long they could communicate silently.

"We don't want you to worry, Cira," Rachel began. Her fingers smoothed her gray wool skirt.

"I already am." I tried to keep from shouting. Their fear filled the limo.

"Bertram went to Atlanta to shut down one of the trafficking rings," Isaac began.

"He told me. So what went wrong?" The cats howled both from the emotions and the fact they hated riding in a car.

"We're not sure," Isaac honestly shared. "All we know is the hunters who were to back him got stopped. Their tires were shot out and the truck nearly rolled. Luckily, they're all unharmed."

"Means our conflict with the hunters won't resume," Rachel said, with a motherly smile. I appreciated her attempt at comforting me.

"Where's my husband?" I waited for an answer.

Isaac glanced out the window. "Our guess is the Laroes are holding him on the grounds somewhere."

"So, we can go in and rescue him, right?" I prayed the option existed.

"It's not that simple." Isaac sighed. "The Laroes are very powerful. If we try to mount a rescue and fail, our actions could ignite a conflict engulfing the entire North and Southeast. There's no telling how many vampires and hunters would be killed."

"So we just leave him there?" I couldn't believe it. I'd uprooted my entire life to be with a man I'd finally figured out I'd fallen in love with, and now some southern family I had never heard of wanted to destroy my future with him. That just wasn't acceptable. "There's a plan right?"

Isaac shook his head. "No."

"What do you mean no?" I couldn't believe no rescue plan had been formed.

"I mean no." He leaned forward as if to impress the importance of his words on me. "We Elders have to keep the peace. I personally agreed with Bertram's plan, but he knew if he failed what the price might be."

"So I could lose my husband?" The full impact on my life had just begun to sink in. My hands started to shake and I fought the urge to cry.

"It'll be all right, Cira," Rachel reassured me as she patted my back. "Bertram is clever. He'll figure out a way to escape."

"Rachel," her husband warned. "Don't give the child false hope."

Child? I hadn't been one of those for many years. Heavens, I was old enough to be approaching grandmother age.

"You think…they'll kill him." I didn't want to say the words.

"I can't be sure. What I do know, he won't be in good shape if he does survive."

~ * ~

One of their airport contacts called Jake the moment she spotted Paul go through security at DIA and head for a gate. The woman had batted her eyes at him to distract him so she could get a good look at his ticket. He'd chosen the cheapest flight possible, with a couple of stops, and it would take over eight hours for him to reach Boston.

One quick call to Lance would assure the hunters would pick up the trail when the man landed. They'd do all they could to protect Mrs. Hoel and he had no doubt, Lance's first call would be to Isaac Rosen.

They just needed to figure out how her ex was discovering information and wreaking havoc.

~ * ~

The phone rang as the driver turned down the street to our home. Isaac answered, his emotions giving him away. With a grim expression he disconnected and looked at me. "Your ex-husband, Paul, is on his way to Boston."

Great, what else could go wrong? I frowned wondering how he'd known where I'd gone. "How long before he arrives?" I inquired.

"We have at least eight hours or a little more."

"I have no idea if he knows where our house is or not."

"Not to worry," Isaac assured me. "You will be protected."

"I'm more worried about my husband than myself." Was Bertram even still alive? If so, what type of torture would he face? Would he be the same man I'd fallen in love with if, no *when*, he returned home?

"The best thing we can do for you both is to make certain you stay safe." Isaac reached across and touched my arm as the car stopped. "He needs a reason to live."

I nodded, trying not to cry. The driver opened the door and carried my luggage and boxes to the front door. Isaac and Rachel accompanied me, each bringing a carrier. I put everything just inside, after disconnecting the security system, and turned to thank Bertram's two oldest friends.

"We're here if you need us," Rachel assured me. "Please do not hesitate to give us a call." She gave me quick hug.

"As soon as your ex lands, we'll let you know" Isaac promised. "In the meantime, I will arrange for your home to be watched and guarded. You'll never see them, but they'll be there."

"I appreciate all your help." All I wanted to do was to throw myself onto my bed and cry. I didn't care for how long.

"Please," Rachel pleaded. "If you need us, don't hesitate."

"If I do, you'll be the first I call," I promised. *Is it rude to wish your guests would leave?*

They both headed out to the limo, and I watched as it drove down the narrow street. Returning inside, I took the carriers upstairs to our bedroom and opened the wire doors. Anghel and Sophie both hesitated before gingerly stepping out, jumping back at any unexpected object.

Exhausted and emotionally overloaded, I threw myself on the satin spread, grabbing Bertram's pillow. I inhaled his scent and felt like a part of my heart had been ripped out. Tears began to flow. Still amazed me vampires cried real tears.

As I cried, I felt two small, furred bodies bump against me, before settling down. They washed themselves first, then snuggled close purring. I hugged my husband's pillow soaking it. After a time I must have slept.

In the twilight place I walked, hearing my footsteps echo. I heard rustling and squeaking, and felt a deep cold penetrate into my bones. The stench of blood filled my nose and broken bodies reeking of human waste littered the ground.

I saw a young woman glance up from her meal, releasing the body, not caring if it hit the dirt. Her eyes met mine. "You shouldn't be here."

"Where is here?" My words seemed to bounce against flower papered walls, yet I knew decay crawled underneath.

"Get out!" another woman ordered.

A sense of tumbling and landing on hard ground. I pushed myself up, hearing chains rattle and pain filled moans. No light penetrated the darkness. Still my eyes could see every detail. Stacked boxes, mold escaping out the top of sacks, and a shape slumped against a wall.

"Who?" The shape moved.

"Bertram?" Was I really seeing him?

I tried to run to him. My feet refused to move and the twilight overtook me, pulling me away.

With a scream I sat up. The cats darted off the bed and I heard their hearts hammer as they sought a hiding place.

Vampires didn't dream. I knew that. Yet somehow I had travelled to the place where my husband had been imprisoned. How was that possible?

My body ached and I stumbled into the bathroom to run hot water over me. When I finished, I tossed on my fleece housecoat and returned to our bed. My cats had claimed a spot and they slept. No doubt exhausted from their harrowing plane and car ride.

Easing myself down, I tried to sort out the images I'd seen. They made no sense. Or rather, I had no context to attach them to so they would.

Dark had fallen and I prayed what I had seen had been true. It meant Bertram still lived. I so desperately wanted him back. What actions could I take to bring him home?

~ * ~

Blood need must be producing hallucinations Bertram decided. He thought he'd seen his wife standing nearby. Her figure had been clear before she'd vanished.

He rested the back of his head against the concrete wall, his wrists burning and his thirst beginning to become more desperate. Even if one of the rodents got close enough, he would not be able to grab and drain it. The thought repulsed him. He hated how they tasted.

Once before he'd been forced to survive off them, right after the quakes. He remembered the ground violently shaking. Rumors later said the Mississippi ran backwards. Modern scientists had more accurately described what happened, but Bertram knew well the death toll had been worse than recorded.

"How are you doing, Dr. Hoel?" Mr. Laroe stood before him holding a goblet full of blood. "Thirsty?" He brought the craved liquid close and momentarily, Bertram thought they might feed him.

He howled, enraged, when the southerner pulled it away and gulped the contents. "Just as you tried to deprive us of our rightfully purchased food, so shall we do with *you*." He laughed as he left.

Alone, in the dark, his hunger becoming uncontrollable, his wrists aching and feeling as if flames engulfed them, Bertram despaired and wanted to, for the first time, sample true death.

Chapter 16

Elder Justice

Lance watched from his vantage point on the Hoel's roof. Lurking in the cobbled street Cira's ex, Paul, whom he recognized from a photo Jake had sent, huddled in a doorway trying to be invisible. The stupid man wasn't. Lance wanted to laugh, even as he pulled his heavy coat tighter with a nervous glance at the sky.

Billowing clouds hovered. The prediction called for a heavy snowfall between six to twelve inches. If blizzard conditions existed, and he suspected they would, the city would begin to shut down as employers sent their employees home. Of course, that only added to the traffic congestion on the roads and increased the number of riders on the T.

His eyes saw a flicker and he concentrated on where he'd seen it. The area seemed clear and he thought maybe he'd imagined movement. Too many hours spent watching the street. He swore he knew every rat who lived there and where they hid.

Movement again and he knew it hadn't been his imagination. A dark shape glided over the roadway, hugging the shadows. Could be a vamp seeking the bounty on Cira's ex. He'd heard Isaac had posted one when the man evaded both the hunters and vamps at Logan Airport.

Only reason he hadn't killed the man and claimed the reward was he didn't want to have to face his children everyday knowing he'd murdered another human, even one who had managed to hack into the hunter's computer records and use the information to murder vamps.

Keeping watch allowed him to make certain Cira Landon Hoel stayed safe from the one living person who had reason to harm her.

The vamp moved again, pausing not far away, stalking like a cat would a mouse. He knew some liked the thrill of the hunt. Lance wondered if the blood tasted better and made a disgusted face. Truth be told, he never wanted to know.

Slowly the creature inched forward, eyes locked on its prey. The man never even noticed. He rubbed his cold hands and blew on them, shuffling back and forth trying to keep warm.

A hand reached out, snagging the human's shoulder, yanking him back against the stone wall. He heard a shriek and the vamp clasped a hand over the man's mouth. The ex tried to plunge a knife into the stomach of his attacker.

Problem was, the vamp proved faster, knocking the knife away and burying teeth into the human's throat. He struggled briefly before his brown eyes glazed over and his body slid slowly to the ground as his blood was drained away. Expertly, two hands snapped his neck. Lance heard the crack.

The killer whirled pinning him with their red eyes. Before they cleared, he recognized Deborah Metcalf. She gave him a bow and tossed her victim over her shoulder. Snow began to fall, and he watched as the Elder disappeared into the storm's fury.

Cira called to him from the roof door. "Lance, please come inside. We don't want you getting sick."

"Coming, Mrs. Hoel." He trotted across the roof space, seeing the deck chairs stacked neatly and the tables turned on their sides. Ducking inside, he immediately felt the warmth. "Surprised you have the heat on."

"Unlike my husband, I still feel the cold." She went down the stairs and he followed. "Will you be returning home before the storm gets worse?"

"No." No need to tell her he'd sent his family away until Lance thought it safe for them to return. He knew enough about what had happened in Atlanta to want to keep his family hidden. The Laroes needed to be dealt with.

Granted, one threat had just been eliminated and should ease the tension between the vamps and hunters.

"I thought I saw Deborah Metcalf," Cira said as they reached the main level.

"You did." With any luck, she hadn't seen anything else.

"If you like, there are guest rooms." She pointed down a hall painted antique white. "Feel free to choose one."

She headed up to the second floor and stopped. "There's food in the kitchen if you're hungry."

"Appreciate it." He pulled off his coat, hat and gloves. "Thanks, Mrs. Hoel."

"Please call me Cira. I chose not to take my husband's last

name."

"And he agreed to that?" He couldn't see a vamp as old as Dr. Hoel allowing it.

A slight smile touched her thin lips. "I didn't give him a choice."

~ * ~

I returned to my office on the third floor. Snow fell outside and I watched the thick flakes gather strength, obscuring my normal view of the bay. When Bertram had replaced the windows during the renovation, he'd put in very good ones. Cold did not seep in and make the room too chilly to work in.

Sitting back at my glass covered desk, I tried to concentrate on the story I'd been working on, only to find my mind wandering away. Getting back on my feet, I stood looking outside as the familiar sights I'd grown so used to vanished behind an endless thick white.

How many people would be allowed to go home, I wondered. Would the stores close as they had when I'd lived here so long ago? Or perhaps Boston had become like the west and would carry on despite the weather until some got trapped in the city, having to seek shelter for the cold stormy night rather than being at home in their familiar bed surrounded by family.

Family. I hadn't had that in a long while. Both my parents had passed and I'd never been close to my siblings. Made me wonder if they'd even noticed I'd gone missing.

Faint smells of cooking food reached my nose. I smiled glad Lance had made himself at home. At least I wasn't the only one here. Funny, Bertram didn't have servants. He only had a housekeeper who came in twice a week to vacuum, dust, wash the linens and clothes. I preferred to wash my own and the woman had been surprised. At least she hadn't argued.

My cell rang and I picked it up. Lucky I had been charging it in my office. "Hello."

"Hello, Mrs. Hoel," a southern accented voice greeted.

"Who is this?" I demanded.

"My name is Jackson Leroe."

"You're the vampire holding my husband." My eyes looked out at the snowstorm, my soul feeling as cold as the freezing temperatures. "What do you want?"

"You want your husband back; therefore you'll give me exactly what I ask for."

I heard a whispering noise and turned to look at the door. Deborah Metcalf stood there, the hem of her long brown dress soaked. She placed a finger on her lips. With a nod I let her know I understood.

"And that is?" I played along.

"Martelli had a second shipment sitting on the dock. You will find the container and bring it to us."

"How am I supposed to do that?"

"I believe your husband received a copy of the legal documents from our supplier's lawyer. My sources tell me the information is there."

Deborah mouthed 'Proof of Life.'

"Before I go digging around in legalese, I want proof my husband is still alive."

"It would serve no purpose to kill him."

"You'll let me talk to him or you can starve." I had no intention of allowing him access to a bunch of innocent humans.

He laughed. "Oh, Mrs. Hoel, it is your husband who is starving." His tone became menacing. "Bring me my cargo that I've paid for and I'll let you take him home."

"I want to talk to Bertram." Two of us could play this game. "I don't get to, I do nothing." I prayed my stubbornness hadn't just killed my husband.

"You stand your ground. I like that. One moment."

I listened carefully for any hint of what was going on. Deborah slipped out the room returning with the bundle of legal papers from Martelli's attorney. She sat down and began going through them.

Leroe came back. "Here he is. Do bear in mind he may not be coherent. It's your wife, Dr. Hoel."

"Cira," Bertram rasped. "Give him noth…"

"Now, now, none of that," the vampire chided. "You have your proof. Now bring me my shipment."

"It's going to take time. Promise me you'll feed him."

"He'll be fed when I get what I want." The line went dead. I stared at my phone and muttered a few choice words, relieved Bertram at least still lived.

"I envy the freedom women have today. Wasn't like that in my time," Deborah commented staring at papers spread across my desk. "I'll call John and have him go through these. He may find the information more quickly than we can."

John, I'd forgotten he was her cousin. Bertram had called him Travis.

She pulled a phone out of an inner pocket. I noticed a bit of blood on her cloak and wisely didn't ask about it. "John, we need you to go through Martelli's documents. We're looking for a cargo container." She listened and nodded. "Yes, filled with humans. Thanks for helping." She grinned at my questioning expression. "Yes, I have a cell phone. So much easier than sending letters by coach or horseback."

I couldn't help but laugh. "Guess I'd never thought about it."

"You aren't from my time." Her eyes darted over more documents. "There's good reason my descendants can't find my grave or death certificate."

"I won't ask."

"You should." Her eyes locked with mine. "You're one of them."

~ * ~

More pain. His wrists and hands ached. His stomach felt as if a fire had been lit and someone kept adding more wood until it burned so hot he could barely stand it. His veins, getting dry, craved blood and he eyed the rat rooting around a bag hungrily.

He strained against the chains, his movement causing more pain. Screaming followed and it took time to realize the sound came from his raw throat. Leaning against the freezing wall, Bertram wanted to die and wondered how he could manage to end his life.

Had he really heard Cira's voice? He prayed he had. At least he'd spoken to her one more time. He had not doubt Leroe intended to kill him.

Leaning his head back, he dropped into the twilight world seeking any kind of escape.

Bertram stood in the upstairs hallway of his home. Moving forward, he seemed to fly until he reached the bedroom door, walking through the wood. Cira lay on the bed, her eyes closed, her two cats beside her, one near her head and other drooped over her legs.

"Bertram?"

He turned to the figure behind him. "What have they done to you?"

Cira came to him, her specter hands reaching for him.

His eyes darted back to the bed assuring himself she still slept there. Turning back to the spirit form, he frowned, not understanding how this could be.

"I don't understand it either." Her ghostly fingers brushed his face. "You need to trim your beard."

"I wish I could hold you." He reached for her. Cira came to him willingly, resting her head on his shoulder although he couldn't feel her.

"I miss you."

"And I you."

Her cat's raspy tongue licked sleeping Cira's face. "No!" she cried as her form vanished. Her body lying in the bed gasped and sat up. "Bertram?" Her eyes searched the room.

Before he could answer, he woke in the cellar, parched, burning from the inside out, weaker than he'd ever been. The rat nibbled at his foot. He stomped it, hearing the bones break as the rodent squeaked. If he could reach it, he could at least get a little blood.

"None of that." Laroe kicked the carcass across the room. "You don't eat until I get my merchandise."

Chapter 17
Unraveling Documents

"Found it!" Travis shouted triumphantly. We'd been searching through the papers for several days.

"About time, John," Deborah replied with a teasing smile.

I could tell they were related just by the way they talked to each other. We'd been in my office, unless we required rest, since Laroe had called, going through every document Martelli had left behind. Even Isaac had spent some time helping out. He'd gone home a couple hours earlier to be with Rachel.

"Well, we had over a hundred years of documents to search through." Travis shook his head. "It's a wonder we found anything."

From what we had learned, Bertram had his work cut out for him to unravel Martelli's criminal empire. His goal may take the next two hundred years. I wasn't sure I wanted him to spend so much of his or rather our lives to complete the task he'd set for himself.

Travis must have read my expression. "You don't care if he succeeds or not."

"I'd rather we do other things with our time."

Deborah shook her head. "Newlyweds."

I hadn't been thinking of bedding my husband. More about traveling the world I had read about or seen on TV. What would it be like to walk the streets of London or see the pyramids in Egypt or gaze upon the Great Wall of China?

"Now," Travis said, pulling out his phone. "We call Isaac, find the container and make a plan."

"Laroe is going to want me to deliver it." I had resolved I'd make the delivery.

"If his shipment is even still alive," Travis reminded me. "They may be dead and don't forget the storm we had a few days ago. Those temperatures alone..."

"I hope not." If they were, Bertram might perish. Not that I had any intention of delivering Laroe's shipment. "If they are dead, can we get rid of the evidence without law enforcement finding out, Travis?" I hated having to ask the question.

"That's the easy part." He made his call. "Isaac, when you get this message, join us at your yacht. We found what we've been looking for." He hung up. "He'll probably get it in the next few hours. I don't know about anyone else, but I'm starving."

Deborah brightened. "I'm up for a hunt, John. Care to join us, Cira?"

"You two go ahead." I wanted to take a shower. My hands were covered in dust and I just felt grimy.

They both left my office, and I faintly heard the front door close. With a sigh I went to the master bath, soaking underneath the hot water, washing the feeling of being covered in filth away and watched as it went down the drain. Tossing on a flannel gown and my housecoat, I sat on the bed. All I wanted to do was cry.

A light knock sounded and I frowned before remembering Lance had been staying with me. "Come in."

"Sorry to bother you, Mrs. Hoel."

"Please call me Cira, Lance."

He frowned, his eyes searching my face. "You're too pale. When's the last time you fed?"

I shook my head. "I don't remember."

"You aren't going to do your husband any good if you don't keep up your strength."

He moved across the hardwood floor and sat beside me working at his sleeve. "Here." His arm appeared in front of me.

"I can't." I tried to push his arm away.

"You can. I'm offering."

I felt wrong to take blood from him after the way he continued to protect me. My hands shaking, I took his wrist and elbow in my hands and bit him. I heard him grunt. Slowly I drank, knowing I had to control my hunger or I might accidentally kill him. I licked the wound when I finished, knowing I had taken much less than I needed.

"If you need more," he began.

"No. I took what I needed," I assured him, despite my craving for more.

His fingers ran over where I'd bit him. Little evidence remained that I had. "Huh." Rising, Lance swayed a little.

"Drink some juice," I suggested.

"Good idea." He left.

Sitting in our room, despair overtook me. Hopefully, between all of us, we could come up with a plan to rescue my husband. I hoped so. Spending my extended life alone did not appeal to me nor did the pain I knew I would experience if he died.

Chapter 18

Search

How many days had passed, Bertram wondered as his mind, for a few seconds at least, cleared. Rodents scurried around him and his mouth watered, wanting to taste them, no matter how disgusting the taste. He needed to feed.

His insides felt twisted, squeezed, causing pain like he'd never felt, not even when he'd been mortal. He groaned, slumping against the very cold wall, the stench of his unwashed body clogging his nostrils.

The outside door opened, bright sunlight invading the darkness of the cellar. He blinked rapidly, trying to see who had come to torment him. A shadow moved toward him.

"I wanted to see how you were faring."

Voice. Female. Ruth Laroe then.

"Fine," he replied. The effort hurt his throat and chest.

"I doubt that." She stood several feet away and he couldn't clearly see her. "You smell."

"Forgive me. I have no choice."

"Perhaps I should have my boys hose you down." She cackled, as if the image pleased her. "The great Dr. Bertram Hoel, world respected scientist, friend of how many world leaders?" She stepped closer. "Reduced to a stinking mass of flesh."

Even vampire blood would help. He hoped she would step close enough to give him the opportunity to drain her.

"I'm not a fool," she answered as if she read his thoughts. "I won't get close enough so your fangs can satisfy the thirst tormenting you."

"How can you do this?" he croaked.

"All a matter of survival, Dr. Hoel. If your wife meets our demands, we may set you free. Or," Her laugh filled the room. "Maybe we'll give her to you as a snack." She whirled and retreated, the doors shutting in a final deafening crash.

"No!" He pulled against the chains holding him, his wrists screaming in agony. "No!"

~ 134 ~

His body collapsed, leaving him hanging. His knees cramped and he knew he had to have blood soon, or else the need could send him into a world of madness from which he might not be able to escape.

~ * ~

Travis drove us to an exclusive marina located in East Boston. Resting in the water sat all manner of yachts, varying in size and I'd guess luxury. Pulling into a spot, he parked and we got out. Deborah led the way. She must have been here before.

I had to fight vertigo as we stepped out on the gray weathered docks. Since I'd never learned to swim, I feared drowning. Granted, I was a vampire and perhaps my fear had no grounds.

"You all right, Mrs. Hoel?" Lance asked.

"Fine." I followed Deborah and Travis.

"Here we are," Deborah announced as she climbed a ladder up onto a light-yellow yacht much smaller than I would have expected Isaac Rosen to own.

The ship bobbed slightly, and I touched the wall as I followed our guide around the outside to the back. Isaac sat here, along with Jacob. I wondered why Rachael or Naomi weren't there.

"From what Travis told me," Isaac said, not bothering with niceties, "we need to locate a certain cargo container."

I nodded, not saying anything, feeling slightly dizzy.

"I already have people on the ground searching," Lance informed the vampire leaders. "Thanks to the information Travis provided, we should find it in a few hours."

"Provided," Jacob interjected. "The information you found, Travis, is correct."

"I have no doubt it is." His laughter contained no humor. "Martelli was a clever one. Kept all his records written and got very good at hiding information."

"We do have a plan," Deborah added, a grin on her face.

Lance nodded. "Dr. Hoel is highly respected. I have more volunteers to rescue him than I have room for."

"Room for?" Isaac's gaze swept across all of us.

I finally spoke. "I'll leave Travis and Lance to explain it to you. If you'll excuse me." I retreated the way I'd come, off the yacht and to the dock. I'd always had motion sickness on boats and it seemed even as a vampire, I still did.

"Are you all right?" Deborah asked, her arm around my waist.

"Just seasick."

"Let's get you back to the car. The men can handle this."

"In this day and age, you know how sexist that sounds?"

"They've had centuries of experience and Lance, well, I think Isaac is watching him."

"For what?" We'd almost reached land.

"He'd make a good vampire one day," Deborah said as if it should be obvious.

"That happen often? A hunter becomes a one of us?" Back on shore my stomach calmed down.

"More often than you'd think despite our agreement. Nothing in it preventing a voluntary turning." She opened the car door and urged me to sit. "John was one such."

"A hunter?" I asked, not certain I had followed her correctly.

"His job as a lawyer always had him traveling. He found out about me and came to kill me. Poor dear." She chuckled. "Had no idea using a stake wouldn't work. Those old legends are so ridiculous."

"Did he become one of us willingly?" I heard myself ask.

"Not so willingly. Didn't matter in the end. He discovered how useful being a vampire was. Helped found a new nation and he always made sure to wear wigs."

I remembered reading powdered wigs had been popular during the seventeen hundreds. No one would have caught on about his real age. Had to wonder when he'd left his family, particularly his beloved Abigail. How had he managed to vanish from history dead and properly buried?

"John is a lawyer and kept up to date on changes. Got good at changing his identity."

"You read minds, Deborah?"

"Just reading your expression, Cira. I've had a couple centuries of practice."

I saw the two men in our party approaching and Isaac's yacht pulling out. Deborah noticed them too. "So now it begins." She grinned. "This will be the most massive operation we've ever mounted with the hunters."

~ * ~

Later in the early evening, Lance covered his face with a kerchief his wife always hounded him to make certain he carried. He missed his family, but glad she'd instilled the habit. The overwhelming stench coming from the container had even the vampires retreating and covering their noses.

"We're too late." Travis shook his head. Odd to see the normally well-dressed attorney in jeans and a long-sleeved plaid shirt.

"Not completely." Lance watched as several hunters, all trained medical personnel, began going through the dead. They lifted a couple of children, getting them on stretchers and into the back of waiting ambulances.

"We'd hoped to rescue more." Travis lifted his walkie-talkie to speak to Isaac and Jacob. The two Elders still remained on the yacht and a few miles out, well away from the main shipping lanes. He gave them a short report.

"Can't bother to get their hands dirty?" Lance couldn't help the jab.

"Not everything is as it seems," Travis answered. Nice generic response Lance supposed. "We've arranged for the burial of the dead."

"You're not going to return them to their families? They deserve closure."

"Would you?" The lawyer pointed at the decayed mess. "Look at the condition of the bodies."

Lance had seen them. He understood the concern, yet thought their families had the right to bury them.

"I'll handle the families," Travis promised. "They will have closure."

"What are you going to do with them?"

"Better you don't know." He sighed, sadness in his dark eyes. "Rescue those you can. The rest, leave to us."

Lance made a face, deciding not to argue. He'd keep the agreement and the peace. His family deserved the chance to grow up without the fear of being killed by vampires.

For now at least.

~ * ~

"They rescued about six children and two adults," Travis reported to his cousin Deborah.

We sat in our main living room; the walls painted white. Bertram had the old-fashioned blue furniture clustered near the hand carved fireplace. My hand stroked the soft fabric as I mourned all those lost lives. "They all had rare blood types?"

He nodded. "We gave them a decent burial."

Deborah looked sad. "That's good."

"What about their families?" I demanded.

"I'm handling it," Travis promised. "They will have a sense of peace about what happened."

"But not the right to bury their dead." It made me angry the Elders could make such a cold-hearted decision.

"It's for the best." Deborah lightly touched my arm. "Believe me, my dear."

"You wouldn't want their bodies returned to their families." John, Travis, looked pale. "Not in the condition we found them. We're using blood types and DNA samples to ID them."

"Oh." If they were using such methods, the bodies must be bad. I still didn't like it though.

"So where is our plan?" My husband's life still hung in the balance, if they hadn't killed him already.

"Truck is on its way to Georgia," his attorney assured me.

I got up and went to stand next to the fireplace, my fingers tracing the intricate pattern carved in the gleaming deep brown wood. "I need to be there."

Deborah shook her head. "Isaac thinks it too dangerous to put you into the Laroe's hands."

"They may kill Bertram if I'm not."

Travis looked at his cousin." She's right, Deborah. You told me you overheard the phone call."

"I do not like the idea of putting a child of our blood in the path of danger." Deborah glared at him.

"You both need to stop treating me as if I were a child needing protection."

They both looked at me surprised.

"You're right," Travis agreed. "Even my own wife could defend our home if needed."

Deborah started to protest.

"Enough!" I'd had it with their coddling. "I'm going to call my pilot. You," I pointed at Travis. "Arrange for me to meet the truck in

Atlanta."

"Consider it done."

"And you," I turned to Deborah. "Go back to the Elders and keep them updated on our progress."

"They are not going to like you going down there." She leaned forward, her eyes burning red.

"I could care less." I wanted my husband back and I'd do anything to get him home, even put my own life in danger. Funny, I had never felt that way about my first husband Paul. I shook my head. That no longer mattered. The man had made his decision and my old life was long behind me.

"Well, get going, both of you."

"As soon as I've made the arrangements, I'll call you with the details." Travis headed for the door. "Come on, Deborah."

"Coming." She rose and bowed slightly. "You have more courage than I would have thought."

"Thank you." I'd take the offhand compliment. They both let themselves out and I glanced around the empty room. Lance was one of those driving the truck down the coast to Atlanta. He was a good man. We'd need him.

Making the call to my pilot, I arranged for a car to take me to the airport and a sitter to take care of my fur babies. As I waited, I put clothes in a backpack, giving both Sophie and Anghel a good pet as they stared at me with disapproving yellow eyes.

I had no intention of allowing a bunch of southern aristocrats to take away the man I loved. My Irish blood burned, and I knew I would fight for the love of my life.

Chapter 19

Rescue

I have to admit I didn't like the idea of riding in the back of a limo following the truck filled with hunters, armed with swords, daggers and even a few guns. Bullets wouldn't do them much good. Sting like hell maybe, but have no other effect on the vampires at all.

"You all right, Mrs. Hoel?" my driver asked. He'd introduced himself as Hank, a local hunter. His bayonet he'd covered and put on the front seat, ready to use if needed.

"Nervous," I admitted.

"Your husband is a lucky man." He glanced at the rearview mirror. "I'm surprised the Elders let you come."

"I had to fight with them about it." Isaac and Jacob had been furious and were still texting their protests from the yacht as they followed us down the coast. They wanted the hunters to handle the situation as originally planned.

My eyes drifted outside, trying to distract my chaotic thoughts, taking in the tree lined highway. Seemed strange not to see for miles like I had in Colorado and the prairie states.

"Been here before?" Hank asked.

"Years ago." I didn't bother going into detail about a vacation I barely remembered.

"Our scouts are reporting there are gators on the Laroe plantation."

"Does Lance know?"

"Yes."

No surprise there. I remembered a tour I'd taken and seeing all the gators around the property. They'd even set up stations where the reptiles could sun themselves.

"We've got two pickups full of locals who will be joining us. They're fifteen minutes behind."

"That wasn't part of the plan."

"Help is gonna be needed with the gators. Once they smell blood, we're expecting them to attack."

"But you don't know."

"Best to be prepared."

Considering how large the beasts could become, backup wasn't the worst idea. I sighed. "How much longer?"

"We turn off the highway in a few miles, then some backroads. Probably a couple of hours." He patted his weapon. "Looking forward to using this."

I cringed. He sounded so gleeful and I had to shut out his excitement.

"Might want to get some rest, Mrs. Hoel. Once the fighting starts, you will need to be at your best."

"And hope none of locals think I'm a target."

"They've been given your picture and your husband's as well. The Elders issued a warning. Nothing is to happen to the two of you."

"Reassuring." I said, not feeling completely confident.

"We'll make sure you get back home safe and sound," Hank promised. "We've known about the Laroes for a long time. Couldn't move against them without the Elders' blessing." He sounded bitter and resentful. I suppose I would too if I knew the Elders could kill me and maybe my family.

"Close the window if you would, please," I requested, listening as the darkened window between me and driver closed. More trees passed and I closed my eyes dropping into the twilight.

I stood before a double door, a heavy plank holding it closed. My fingers removed the obstacle and I descended down the cellar steps. Rats rose up on their hindquarters, their beady eyes looking at me and their noses twitching.

Chained to the wall a skeletal man groaned, his eyes sunken into his skull, his clothes in tatters and the smell coming off of him made me gag. How I knew this was my husband, I had no idea. Slowly I approached.

He jumped at me, the chains rattling, his eyes wild and fingers scratching the air. Growls came from him and red spittle dribbled out of his mouth.

"Bertram?" My voice shook. *Dear God! Were we already too late?*

He struggled against the confines holding him.

"Bertram, we're coming. Please, my love, please, hold on."

His eyes scrunched closed and he shook his head. His eyes cleared. "Cira?"

"We're in the twilight place."

He sagged. "You're not really here."

"I'm not." She dared to step closer. "We're coming, Bertram. We're coming."

~ * ~

"We're coming, Bertram. We're coming," echoed in his mind. Bertram barely held onto his sanity, knowing how dangerously close he was to losing the battle. Much longer and they'd have no choice except to put him down. He almost wanted a merciful end.

And a nightmare for Cira. The bond would break between them. Not just the love they shared but also physical. She'd mourn him and her entire body would hurt. Why hadn't he told her the full consequences of a Blood Marriage? His wife had right to know and he hadn't told her!

How stupid could he have been?

"Hold on," he whispered. "Hold on. They're coming."

The words became a mantra, the only thing he had to cling to. He had to hold on. Bertram couldn't put Cira through the agony he knew she would feel if he died the final death.

He couldn't.

"Hold on," he told himself again and again and again, even as he felt his sanity slipping further and further away as the blood lust took full control and all he could think of was draining the next human or vampire who came to him.

~ * ~

The beautiful house came into view. Painted white, it stood out from the tall trees and colorful pink magnolias that seemed to be everywhere in the south. Their sweet smell greeted me. I sat up and didn't miss the ponds with gators sunning themselves on the banks or platforms.

The truck stopped a few feet away, the limo coming to stop close behind.

"We're here," Hank informed me.

Not really needing to be told I thanked him and waited as he opened the door before I got out. I wore a simple blue dress and practical flats. If I needed to run, I wouldn't have to stop and take my shoes off. I never understood why in the movies women always wore heels.

A woman came out the door fanning herself. Her overconfident smile told me I would be dealing with a cunning opponent. She took the stairs and approached, her greedy eyes looking first to the truck before focusing on me.

"Welcome to my home," she greeted, using her southern accent to her advantage or so she thought. Absently she patted her blonde hair, her red skirt floating over the ground. "I'm Ruth Laroe."

"Hello," I answered. "I'm Cira Landon Hoel."

"We've been expecting you."

I tried not to start when a giant gator, much bigger than I've ever heard about, came around the corner of the house and waddled past the porch.

"That's just the Major. He's been here for longer than any of us remember."

"He's good sized."

She laughed. "Good appetite too."

A chill ran down my spine. No need to use my imagination regarding how they got rid of their victims' bodies.

I pulled my mind away from the horrific image. Bertram needed my help.

"I want to see my husband."

"First things first." She turned to the truck. "Open it up."

Lance and another man I didn't know undid the padlock and opened the door. Inside sat bodies crowded together, mostly men, but a few women. A wail drifted out and I wondered who had voiced the sound. The hunters certainly were doing a good job of acting like frightened captives.

"Where are the children?" Her angry red eyes glared at me.

"They didn't survive. We brought what did." She had no idea what actually had happened.

"Disappointing." Her foot tapped the ground.

"My husband?" I prompted again.

"Oh, he's safe enough." She pointed at Lance. "Unload them."

He started helping some of the women. They kept their eyes down.

"Put them in the barn over there." She pointed at a wood building opposite the house. I noticed several workers in the field. "My husband and sons will attend them."

I could see three figures waiting. Feeling uneasy, I glanced at Lance. He gave a slight shake of his head.

"Come, my dear." She motioned toward the house. "I so rarely have company. Won't you join me for a cup of tea?"

"Thank you for your hospitality, but since I have fulfilled my part of the bargain, I want to see my husband."

She pushed her lower lip out pouting, a very unbecoming look for a woman of her age. "If you insist. I had the boys hose him off earlier." Ruth headed off toward the side of the house.

Before I followed, I checked to see where everyone was. Hank leaned against the car, his eyes on the horizon, probably waiting for the reinforcements. Lance and the others shuffled toward the barn.

"You were in such a hurry to see your husband, don't doddle," Ruth griped.

"Sorry. Got distracted." The gator had stopped close to the hunters and seemed to be very interested in them.

Mrs. Laroe pulled the heavy bar locking the storm cellar doors and pointed down. "He's there."

I knew this place from the twilight rest I'd shared with Bertram. Her attitude put me on alert. The Laroes had no intention of allowing anyone to leave. "After you." I motioned her to go first.

She hesitated, telling me my sense of her had been correct. "If you insist," she deigned.

"I do."

With a dainty shrug she descended the narrow steps, standing at the bottom, poised to flee back up and lock me in.

The room stank. Rats and mice nibbled and scurried over rotting food. Bertram stood chained to the wall, wet clothes hanging on him, his eyes red and wild. He snarled.

"Or course, I can't guarantee he won't drain you." She pushed me toward him and turned to run up the stairs.

"Oh, no you don't." I grabbed her long skirt and dragged her back. "You didn't think I'd prepared for this?" I pushed her toward my husband, hearing gunfire in the distance and the sound of truck brakes screeching.

Ruth's eyes widened. She clawed at me. I ducked her attempted attack, managing to grab her arm and twist it behind her back. Mrs. Laroe yelped. "Let me go, you little tramp!"

"Tramp?" I laughed at her, forcing her across the filthy floor.

Bertram excitedly shook his chains, his hungry eyes looking at us both. Just how dangerous he'd become hit me along with the overwhelming sense of need and bloodlust he broadcasted.

How could I as a loving wife, deny him what he needed most?

"Where the hell are the chain keys?" I demanded.

"Peg on the wall."

I needed to reach them and not have Mrs. Laroe lock us both in.

"Here, Mrs. Hoel." Very human fingers handed them to me, placing his bayonet against Mrs. Laroe's throat. "Give me a reason," Hank warned.

She stopped struggling. I dared to release her and undid one of my husband's arms. As his wrist dropped, I saw red welts and blisters. I had to duck his grab for me and decided I dared not completely release him.

"He's hungry," I said backing away.

Hank grinned. "Well, good thing we can feed him." He shoved Ruth Laroe at my husband, who deftly caught her and managed to sink his fangs into her throat. She gave a strangled cry, stiffening, before her body went slack.

Bertram dropped her. I could feel his still burning hunger.

I heard a mournful "No!" from the stairs and a young man I didn't know launched himself at Bertram. Hank pushed me out of the way and unlocked the other chain. The hunter grabbed me and dragged me toward the entrance. "Run!"

The sound of their fight followed us outside. I hoped Bertram would be all right.

I took in the struggle going on near the barn and trucks. The gators rushed to feast on the dead. "Get into the house!" Hank ordered, gripping his weapon and rushing into the fray.

I dodged a gator and reached the stairs leading up to the porch. Hurrying inside, I watched the fighters through the screen door. Evidently there were more vampires on the plantation than we knew. They rushed at the hunters from the fields.

"Daddy made an army." I turned to face a young woman who looked much like her mother. She grinned at me a sword in her hand, her tight jeans and cropped top completely out of place in the old-fashioned room. "That's why we needed regular shipments to keep them fed." Moving forward she waved her weapon. "I'm going to take your head just like I've been taught."

I grabbed the door meaning to retreat, when I heard the snapping of jaws. The Major, as Mrs. Laroe called him, stood on the porch, waiting for a meal. Wildly I looked around for an escape.

"No place for you to go," the daughter said, advancing toward me.

I pushed past the young woman, racing through the living room until I reached sweeping stairs. Running up them I heard her footsteps as she rushed after me. Opening the first door I found, I slammed it shut, and ran to the window. Luckily, it gave easily and I crawled onto the roof, ignoring how far the ground seemed.

The woman laughed, leaning out the window as I edged my way across. "All I have to do is wait you out. No place to go."

I worked my way to the brick chimney and huddled against it, as the battle raged below. Bodies fell. I had no idea if they were vampire or human. Gators feasted on the remains. The grass and dirt below slowly got covered in blood. I could smell the tangy scent.

Not able to watch anymore, I hid my face against the structure, terrified to move, praying the blood Bertram received had helped him recover. If not, I shuddered, not liking what the hunters might have to do.

~ * ~

His mind slowly returned to him after he drained the second vampire. While not the best solution to cure bloodlust, it helped revive him. Stumbling out of the cellar and he stared at the mayhem. Humans and vampires fought each other, while alligators feasted on the dead. Blood coated the ground and grass. He could smell the tangy copper and he craved more.

A young woman stormed out of the house waving a sword over her heard, screaming at the top of her lungs. Behind her flames burst the windows and licked slowly up the side. He followed their progression and gasped in horror. Cira huddled next to the chimney trapped.

"No!" He ran across the grounds, dodging the gators. As he reached the porch stairs, Jackson Laroe blocked his path.

The southerner smiled. "Seems only fitting. You took the life of my wife." He slid forward, a sharp blade in his hands. "I will now make certain yours dies." Madness whirled in his eyes. "Pity too, she is such a lovely little thing."

"Let me pass," Bertram growled. "You and I can settle this later."

"Oh, no, Dr. Hoel, we will settle this now."

With a frantic glance upward, he could see the fire licking up the side toward his wife. He heard her scream his name.

"Dr. Hoel!" He saw a flash of silver and caught the sword tossed to him. He nodded his thanks to a hunter.

Laroe smiled. "Excellent. Now the odds will be even." He took up a position. "Shall we duel while your wife burns to death?"

~ * ~

I heard the clashing of swords and dared a quick glance below. My husband and another man fought, their combat dance taking them down the stone walkway and out into the large area where the limo and the truck sat. Several gators snapped at them.

A beam cracked and a portion of the roof collapsed inward causing yellow-orange flames to reach hungrily at the shingles. I gasped unsure when it had started. Like greedy fingers the blaze crept along the eaves coming closer to my perch. My back pushed into the brick as I realized, I had not where to go!

I looked wildly around for an escape. Not far away a tree stood near the chimney.

Another section gave way, dropping to the lower level with a loud bang. Desperate, I knew I'd have to take a chance. I might miss and plunge to the ground. If I broke my neck, I hoped my death came quickly. My loss would be devastating for my husband. I couldn't fathom the agony he'd feel.

Getting to my feet, I edged past the chimney where smoke bellowed out. I coughed, before pushing as hard as I could with my feet, praying I managed to grab a branch. I hung in the air, my hands trying to catch the limb I had aimed for.

I fingers grazed the bark and I held on even as I heard a loud crack and my body plunged toward the ground.

My arms and legs flailed. I closed my eyes, preparing to hit, pretty sure even as a vampire the fall would crush every bone in my body.

Time seemed to stop as I fell. I prepared myself to die, sad to leave the husband I had worked so hard to free.

Instead of the hard earth, I hit something that gave under my weight. I blinked, trying to understand why I hadn't died. I looked up into the grinning faces of Isaac and Jacob Rosen each holding one side of a huge fishing net.

"When did you," I managed, before being helped out by Isaac. My body swayed and he caught me.

"Easy, Cira," Isaac comforted. "You're safe."

"Bertram?" I frantically tried to find him.

"Engaged in a very important duel. Come, we need to move away from the house before it collapses." Supporting me, Isaac helped me away from the house and back to the car. I leaned against the side, trying to process the fact I'd survived.

The sound of metal clashing brought my attention back to the fight going on between Bertram and another man. "Who is he fighting?" I asked Isaac, noticing his cousin Jacob standing beside him.

"Jackson Laroe," Isaac answered.

"His wife, daughter and both sons are dead," Jacob added. "Along with most of the army he'd created. Some fled into the swamp. The gators chased them."

"The hunters?" They'd all been so brave. I had to know.

"Unknown."

I saw Hank assist an injured hunter to the truck, where another used a medical kit to treat the wound. They'd come well prepared.

My eyes darted back to my husband's fight. Laroe had knocked the sword from Bertram's hands and had a triumphant look on his face. "Now you'll die," he promised. "And you wife will know the pain of your death."

I tried to dart forward. Isaac and Jacob both stopped me. I struggled against them. "No!" I screamed.

As the blade came to take Bertram's head, my husband dodged to the side and used his foot to kick Laroe's shin. The other yelled, nearly falling, dropping his weapon. As he reached for it, the Major ambled up and snapped his huge jaws tight about the southerner's middle. I heard a loud crunch and saw the look of complete surprise on the vampire's face, before the reptile toddled across the red ground and toward the pond nearby, vanishing under the water with his prey.

Isaac and Jacob released me. Briefly I stood there, before running to my husband and throwing my arms around him where he knelt, his knees turning crimson. He smelled awful and felt way too thin.

"I'm all right," he reassured me, holding me tight.

"I almost lost you," I choked out.

"You didn't." He got to his feet, pulling me with him. "You need to release me. I still need to feed and I don't want to hurt you."

"But," I objected.

"Cira, please do what I ask for your own safety."

"Come child," Isaac urged. "Your husband is trying to protect you."

My husband sank back to the ground, his whole body shaking.

"What does he need?" Lance asked as he joined us.

"Fresh blood."

Several of the hunters exchanged glances and nodded. Lance kneeled beside Bertram offering his arm. "Take what you need and know there are others willing."

My husband turned his face away. "I can't."

"Of course you can." Lance smiled at me. "I offered the same to your wife and she accepted."

Bertram threw a surprised look at me. I nodded. "Just don't drain any of them. I think they'd behead you if you did."

Chapter 20
Home

Lance watched his children running around and screaming happily in their back yard. His wife joined him, putting an arm around his waist and leaning her head on his upper arm. "It's over?"

"For now."

"Why do you keep doing this, Lance? Surely someone else can take over and free you to live your life."

"My family has been leading the hunters for over a hundred years. It's our destiny."

"Or curse." She pointed at their boys. "Do you expect one of them to replace you?"

He hugged her close. "Only if they want to."

His wife gave him a hopeful expression and he kissed her, knowing his family would always safeguard the agreement made over a century ago and keep the vampires in check.

They owed it to all humanity.

~ * ~

Bertram stared out at the garden, a layer of snow covering the dead plants. He'd fed earlier and felt somewhat better. Isaac had told him it would take time to recover from the combined starvation and poison the Laroe's had subjected him to.

Martelli's papers lay spread across his desk, but he questioned the wisdom of trying to undo a criminal empire the other had so carefully constructed. He'd almost died trying to end just one trafficking ring. What might happen if he tried to end another operation in a more dangerous location, like the several the Italian had going in China or Italy or England?

"Bertram?"

He looked up at his wife standing in the door. She looked lovely in a sweater and a pair of jeans, although he had to smile at the cat slippers she wore. "How are you feeling?"

"Better."

"Are you really or are you just saying that to make me feel better?" Cira sat down on his desk. "Please, tell me you aren't thinking about trying to end anything else." She waved her hand over the papers.

"I'm thinking I may use some of Isaac's contacts in various agencies to put an end to Martelli's empire."

"That's the first sensible thing I've heard you say." She sounded relieved.

"Learned my lesson." He had no desire to come so close to dying again.

"Rachel told me all of it you know. What would happen if you died."

He looked at her concerned face, really seeing her for the first time. "Yet you agreed."

"Did I really have a choice?" She leaned over and kissed him. He pulled her to him, ignoring the papers as they settled on the floor.

"No," he whispered in her ear, wishing he had the strength to make love to her. Not that his office would ever be the right place.

"You promised to tell me what happened between you and Martelli."

He remembered making the promise, yet felt reluctant to tell her.

Her eyes searched his face, her fingers playing in his beard. "Bertram?"

"It was over a woman," he breathed.

"A woman?" She frowned.

He nodded. "A hunter woman. Martelli loved her not realizing she was bait." He sighed and walked over to the window gazing out. "It was before our agreement with the hunters. I killed her to protect him. He never forgave me."

"So that's why he kept trying to…" Cira stopped. He could see her pained expression reflected in the glass.

"He would have taken you from me just as I did the same to him."

"Some of his comments make sense now," she muttered.

"What comments?" he demanded.

"Doesn't matter. He's gone." She changed the subject. "Have you read your email?"

"I'm still catching up." He'd wondered if she'd ever tell him what Martelli had said.

"We've been invited back to the convention where we met. I took the liberty of telling them yes for both of us."

"You want to return? What about your ex, Paul?"

She smiled as if she knew something he didn't. "Let's just say he isn't a concern anymore." A brief flash of sadness crossed her face. "I am sorry he met the end he did."

"What happened to him?"

"Let's just say Deborah took care of it."

Chapter 21
The Day before the Con

I guess I shouldn't have been surprised my husband decided to fly us to the convention the day before it started. As we stood in line to check into the hotel, I glanced around the familiar lobby, remembering the way my life used to be and all the changes which had happened after meeting Bertram last year, including the twelve previous conventions I'd attended at the insistence of my romance publisher and the six writing conferences. Next year already had a full schedule.

Once up in our room, I looked out the window and saw the tall buildings making up DTC with parking lots and employees leaving late, completely unaware of the vampire community surrounding them.

I felt my husband slip his arms around me, pulling me against his body. "We have nothing planned for this evening." I recognized his tone and knew how we'd fill it.

"Don't we?" I teased, turning in his arms and kissing him.

He picked me up and carried me to the bed, his hands exploring my body. Several weeks had passed before we could make love after what happened to him in Georgia. Since then, he'd been very attentive as if making up for time lost.

As we lay together, content and satisfied, he kissed my neck. "I never regretted marrying you."

"Me either," I told him. This change in my life has, surprisingly enough, made me very happy.

"Good. We have many years together, Cira" His fingers traced my cheek. "How would you like to spend them?"

"Traveling," I answered, knowing exactly how to arouse him again. Vampire men have far more stamina than human ones.

"As you wish, my beautiful Blood Bride."

About the Author

Belle Blukat is a Colorado Writer who enjoys writing romance stories between supernatural creatures and humans. Some of her tales happen on Earth while others transpire on other worlds. After all, if humanity travels into space, why would vampires, shifters and others stay behind?

She is writing several series and publishing them on Amazon as short stories or novellas. Blood Bride is her first Paranormal Romance Novel. The tale is set in Denver, CO and Boston, MA where she has lived and outside of Atlanta, GA on plantations she has visited. Yes, Gators do live there.

Looking for something else to read – then check out:

WolfSinger Publications
www.wolfsingerpubs.com

www.ingramcontent.com/pod-product-compliance
Lightning Source LLC
Chambersburg PA
CBHW070751180626
46818CB00007B/3066